'Are you hurt?' Nathan demanded.

Danielle was vaguely aware that the driver had got out of the red car and was staring angrily at her. 'No. Is the dog OK?'

'If it had been on a lead it wouldn't have happened.'

'Oh, it wasn't the dog's fault,' protested Danielle. 'My car backfired. . .and you were driving much too fast for these country roads. . .'

Dear Reader,

Babies loom large this month! Lilian Darcy takes us to the Barossa Valley vineyards in Australia and an obstetric practice, while Margaret Holt's second book takes us back to the midwifery unit at Beltonshaw Hospital. Two aspects of general practice are dealt with by Laura MacDonald and Janet Ferguson, though single doctor practices must be rare now! Hope you like them. . .

The Editor

Laura MacDonald lives in the Isle of Wight. She is married and has a grown-up family. She has enjoyed writing fiction since she was a child, but for several years she has worked for members of the medical profession, both in pharmacy and in general practice. Her daughter is a nurse and has also helped with the research for Laura's Medical Romances.

Recent titles by the same author:

LOVE CHANGES EVERYTHING
ALWAYS ON MY MIND

GYPSY SUMMER

BY

LAURA MacDONALD

MILLS & BOON LIMITED
ETON HOUSE 18–24 PARADISE ROAD
RICHMOND SURREY TW9 1SR

First published in Great Britain 1992
by Mills & Boon Limited

This edition 1992

ISBN 0 263 77843 6

Set in 10½ on 12½ pt Linotron Baskerville
03-9209-47037

Typeset in Great Britain by Centracet, Cambridge
Made and printed in Great Britain

CHAPTER ONE

IT WAS a warm afternoon in early summer, and Danielle Roberts was driving through the Hampshire lanes to her home in the village of Lower Yarrow after two weeks' holiday in Devon. It was one of those idyllic sort of days with a clear blue sky, thick white blossom on the hawthorn hedges on either side of the road and the lush green of the grass verges almost waist-high with cow-parsley.

The engine of her elderly Morris Minor had overheated twice on the journey, and it was with a sense of relief that Danielle saw the welcome signpost that reminded her that she was only half a mile from home. There was no warning of the incident that was to follow, and afterwards she found it difficult to remember the exact sequence of events; she could recall seeing the young boy in the faded blue jeans walking ahead of her on the grass verge, a thin lurcher dog at his side; she remembered seeing the red car as it came round the bend towards her and thinking that it was travelling too fast; and she most definitely remembered hearing the sound, which was like a gunshot, as her own car backfired, but what happened after that was a jumble in her mind.

She could only presume that the dog, startled by the noise, had streaked across the road in front of her, she had swerved to avoid it into the path of the oncoming red car, which in its turn had swerved to avoid her and had ended up on the opposite grass verge, its wheels embedded in the bank. Danielle's car skidded and she slid to a halt, the vehicle slewed sideways across the road.

In the silence that followed the squealing of her tyres she sat very still, gripping the steering-wheel, every nerve taut as she anticipated an impact that didn't come. Then when she realised she was all right and that the boy was still standing on the verge her immediate thought was for the dog. Wrenching open her car door, she almost fell out and hurried across the road.

By this time the driver had got out of the red car and was staring angrily at her. She was vaguely aware of a tall slim man, his hair thick and fair, his clothes casual.

'Are you hurt?' he demanded.

'No.' Her reply was breathless, then she turned to the boy, who had crossed the road and was bending down beside the dog. 'Is the dog OK?' she asked anxiously.

'Yeah, he's just frightened, that's all,' said the boy, squinting up at them through a tangle of thick black hair.

'If it had been on a lead it wouldn't have happened.' The man was obviously still very angry.

'Oh, it wasn't the dog's fault,' protested Danielle. 'My car backfired. . .and you were driving much too fast for these country roads. . .'

'I wasn't blaming the dog,' replied the man, ignoring her accusation. 'It's up to the owner to keep an animal under proper control so that it doesn't cause accidents.' As he spoke he walked round to the front of his car to see if any damage had been done, then, looking over his shoulder at Danielle, he added, 'And don't you think it would be a good idea to move your car before something else comes round that bend and drives straight into it?'

There was a note of sarcasm in his voice, and with a guilty start she turned and hurried back across the road. It was only after she'd started the engine and turned the car, pulling forward and parking at the side of the road, that she realised her hands were shaking. She sat still for a moment and watched as the man reversed his car away from the bank, then climbed out and carefully examined it. By this time the boy had tied a piece of string round the dog's neck and the pair of them were standing silently on the grass verge.

As the man finally straightened up Danielle wound down her window. 'Is there any damage?' she called out.

'Fortunately, no,' he replied, then, turning to the boy, he added, 'Lucky for you. I'd say you've been in quite enough trouble as it is. You'd better get on home, and keep that animal under control in future.'

The boy sidled away, the dog at his side, and Danielle watched as the pair of them crossed the deep grass verge and ducked beneath the overhanging branches of the hawthorn, disappearing from view into the woods beyond. She jumped when she realised the man had spoken to her again.

'I'm sorry,' she called, shading her eyes from the glare of the sun, 'did you say something?'

He sighed, and she got the impression that his anger had given way to irritation. 'I simply asked if your car is all right?'

'I think so, although I have been having trouble—it keeps overheating.'

'Do you have far to go?' He walked across the road towards her, and she noticed he was wearing a white open-necked shirt and a pair of pale blue trousers.

She shook her head. 'No, only into the next village—I think I should make that all right.'

He appeared to hesitate for a moment, then he nodded abruptly and turned away, but not before she had noticed that he was deeply suntanned and that his eyes were very blue.

She watched as he climbed back into his car, wondering if he was always bad-tempered or whether he'd had one of those days where one more incident was simply the last straw. She had the feeling that he would look very different if he smiled, but it seemed as if she wasn't to find that out, for he started the engine and pulled sharply away, and with only another brief nod in her direction he was gone.

Idly she wondered who he was. She'd certainly never seen him before, and she knew most people in the village, if only by sight. She finally came to the conclusion that he was probably only passing through and that no doubt she would never set eyes on him again. And yet. . .she hesitated and stared at the spot beyond the grass verge where the boy and his dog had disappeared. . .there had been something about the way in which he'd spoken to the boy that suggested that they weren't strangers, almost as if they had clashed previously on some recent occasion. Come to that, she didn't know the boy either, although there had been something vaguely familiar about him—his thin brown body, the untidy black hair and the sullen dark eyes.

Thoughtfully Danielle turned the key in the ignition, and as the engine throbbed to life again she glanced in her mirror at the empty road behind her, then gave one last look towards the thick dark woodland beyond the hawthorns before she let out the clutch and headed towards the village and home.

By the time she reached Farthings, her white-washed cottage overlooking the village green, and had taken her bags from the boot of her car she had practically forgotten the incident, especially as Shelley, her long-haired tortoiseshell cat, was on the doorstep to greet her. It was good to be home, in spite of the fact that she had thoroughly enjoyed her holiday with her family in Brixham.

Her cottage seemed hot and stuffy after being shut up for so long, and Danielle went round opening windows to help air the place. She had inherited the cottage two years previously from her grandmother, and at the time she had just finished her general nursing training in a large Wiltshire hospital. It had been her intention to work in dermatology, but when she had visited the village of Lower Yarrow after the death of her grandmother she had found that the local GPs, Drs Griffiths and Maitland, were looking for a practice nurse.

Danielle had spent most of her childhood with her grandmother in Lower Yarrow, as her parents had been working abroad; she loved the place, and when Dr Griffiths, whom she had known most of her life, had offered her the job at his surgery she had needed little persuading. By the time her parents had returned to England and settled in Devon Danielle had been firmly established at Farthings and enjoying her newly found independence.

After she had unpacked her bags in the chintzy bedroom under the eaves she changed from the jeans and shirt she had worn for travelling into a floral-printed skirt and a cool white camisole top.

Then she went downstairs into the cosy flagstoned kitchen with its old-fashioned Aga, rows of gleaming copper pans and bunches of dried flowers and herbs, and, unbolting the back door, she stepped out into the garden—a profusion of colour, but at the same time cool and dense with fresh new foliage.

She took a deep breath, drinking in lungfuls of the sweet early-evening air mingled with the scent of the clematis that climbed over the doorway. After inspecting the lawn, the shrubs that had flowered in her absence, the semi-wild flowerbeds, thick with periwinkle and enormous scarlet poppies, and her precious herb garden beneath the kitchen window, she called across the hedge to her neighbour Bessie, thanking her for taking care of Shelley.

On returning to the kitchen she prepared a salad and a cup of herbal tea. Danielle had been a vegetarian for about a year, and had found the change beneficial in terms of health and vitality. Her thick curly brown hair, which she wore in a jaw-length bob, seemed to have taken on a golden sheen, her clear greeny-grey eyes had a sparkle that she was sure hadn't been there before, and her complexion, which her mother had always insisted on defining as the English rose variety, had a newly found lustre about it.

While she ate her tea she caught up on her mail, then afterwards she sat dreamily for a few moments in the open doorway, staring into the garden and stroking Shelley, who, obviously delighted to have her home again, had jumped up on to her lap.

At last, with a sigh, she glanced at her watch, and as she saw the time she realised that evening surgery would soon be starting. She decided on a sudden impulse that she would go to the surgery and see Elaine, the receptionist, and catch up on all the news.

Just before she had left for Devon Dr Maitland, Dr Griffiths' partner, had been preparing to leave for a trip to Australia and New Zealand with his wife and family. It was to be the trip of a lifetime, and would take about a month. In his absence Dr Griffiths had employed a locum, a Dr Stafford, and Danielle was curious to see how the new arrangement was working out.

She left the cottage and, humming softly to herself, she crossed the village green. The sun was casting long shadows from the huge horse-chestnut trees that dotted the green, their lush branches tipped with red or white flowers like candles on Christmas trees. A group of boys were kicking a football, people were exercising their dogs and a young girl was riding her pony on the wide grass verge at the side of the road. Danielle watched enviously—she too loved to ride whenever she had the opportunity, which wasn't as frequently as she would have liked. One or two people called out or waved to her as she walked. She knew most folk in the village, although in the last year or so there seemed to have been a steady influx of people from town who had either moved to the village to live or who had bought old properties and renovated them for weekend retreats.

As she passed the boys with the football she was suddenly reminded of the boy with his dog, and as she approached Westover, Dr Griffiths' house, in the lane on the far side of the green, she found herself wondering if the suspicions she had had about the boy had been correct.

There were several cars already parked in the drive or in the lane outside the house, where the surgeries were held, but Danielle only gave these a cursory glance as she skirted the main entrance, which the patients used, and slipped round the side of the old building, ducking beneath the overhanging boughs of a lilac bush that tumbled unchecked over the wall.

She entered the house by the side-entrance and

found Elaine in the reception office, talking on the telephone to a patient who had obviously asked for an appointment the following morning. As Danielle put her head round the door Elaine glanced up, and her initial look of surprise was quickly replaced by one of pleasure.

Danielle went right into the room, then, closing the door behind her, she waited while Elaine finished making the appointment.

Elaine was in her forties and had worked for Dr Griffiths for three years. She had been part of the London migration, as Danielle called the many townies who had settled in Lower Yarrow, but Danielle liked Elaine and enjoyed working with her. Times hadn't been easy for Elaine since her husband had been forced into early retirement following a heart attack, but she rarely talked about her problems. As she replaced the receiver she spun round in her swivel chair. 'Well, look who's here, then,' she said. 'When did you get back? Did you have a good time?'

Danielle laughed. 'I got back this afternoon, and yes, I had a lovely time, in spite of having to help my mother with her charity fund-raising.'

'Well, I must say you look well on it. Just look at the colour of you! You'd think you'd been to the Bahamas instead of Devon.' Elaine grinned.

'Yes, it has been hot,' agreed Danielle. 'I hope it's going to continue.'

Elaine turned briefly back to the desk as two patients came in, then after she had told them to take a seat in the waiting-room she turned curiously back to Danielle. 'Did you get the chance to attend that course in Torquay you were on about?'

'The aromatherapy?' Danielle smiled. 'Yes, I did. And it was a good course, although it was only for two days.' She had been interested in aromatherapy for some time now, and had spent a good deal of time studying essential oils and their health-giving properties.

'You'll have to give me a massage some time,' said Elaine. 'My back's been stiff again.'

'Of course.' Danielle glanced round as she spoke. 'How have things been here?'

Elaine shrugged. 'Oh, you know. . .the usual. Dr Maitland got away all right, and Dr Stafford's been taking his surgeries.'

'What's he like?' asked Danielle curiously.

'Quite dishy really,' said Elaine reflectively. 'He's about thirty or so, I should think. But there's something about him that I can't quite put my finger on.'

'What do you mean? His appearance?'

'Oh, no, nothing like that. As I say, he's really quite attractive in a rugged sort of way. No, it's more his manner. . .' she hesitated, then went on '. . .he seems very uptight about something. Apparently he's been working abroad. . .oh, and just in case you should be interested I found out that he isn't married,' she added innocently.

'Elaine, you really are the limit!' Danielle laughed again. 'When are you going to stop trying to pair me off with every male who comes into sight?'

Elaine shrugged. 'When you get yourself settled

down with some nice young man, I suppose,' she replied. 'It isn't right, an attractive girl like you, not being interested.'

'I've never said I'm not interested,' protested Danielle. 'I just haven't met anyone I could imagine spending the rest of my life with—and besides, I quite like my own company, and, let's face it, I am only twenty-three.' Then in an attempt to change the subject she said, 'How's Dr Griffiths?'

Elaine glanced into the hall, then, lowering her voice, she said, 'His stomach's been bad again, so he's been a bit grouchy, but the main problem around here has been the hippies. . .' she added, shaking her head.

'Hippies. . .?' Danielle looked up sharply.

'Yes, haven't you seen them? They appeared suddenly about ten days ago and parked their vehicles on the common—they're a scruffy lot; they've really upset some of the locals. . .' She broke off to answer the phone, and Danielle waited patiently again until she had dealt with the patient's query and had hung up.

'Are you sure they're hippies?' she asked thoughtfully. 'Or are they gypsies?'

'Hippies, travellers, gypsies. . .is there any difference?' Elained sniffed and began filing some patient records in the carousel filing systems.

'Oh, yes,' replied Danielle firmly. 'There most certainly is a difference.'

There must have been something in her tone, for the older woman stopped what she was doing and peered up at her questioningly. 'I didn't know you were an authority on the subject.'

Danielle pulled a face. 'I wouldn't exactly call myself that, but when I was a child there was a group of gypsies who came every year and camped on Farmer Jones's land—they worked in the fields and helped with the strawberry picking. They fascinated me—we village children weren't supposed to play with them, but we all did.'

'But weren't they dirty and smelly?'

'If they were I certainly didn't notice,' said Danielle slowly. 'There aren't many true gypsies left today, but there are still some who have Romany blood in their veins and carry on the old traditions.'

'Well, all this lot seem to have done is cause trouble—there've been fights with the local lads and trouble in the shops in the village,' Elaine rolled her eyes, 'and they can't have come to pick fruit, because Farmer Jones isn't there any more and those fields are all planted with rape-seed now.'

Danielle remained silent, but what Elaine had just said had set her mind working again on her earlier suspicions about the boy with the dog. At the time she had thought there was something vaguely familiar about him. Now her curiosity was further increased and suddenly she felt an impulse to go and see if her suspicions were correct.

'It's Dr Stafford I feel sorry for,' said Elaine.

'Why, what's it got to do with him?'

'Well, he's staying in Dr Maitland's house in the lane that borders the common. He has to put up with them morning, noon and night.' As they had been speaking Danielle had automatically picked up a pile of notes from the desk and had moved round behind the carousel, bending down to file them away.

'I'm sure people make a lot of fuss unnecessarily,' she said. 'I honestly don't know why people can't mind their own business. I'm sure those people aren't doing any harm.'

'But they aren't camped on your doorstep, are they?'

The voice was deep and somehow familiar. Slowly Danielle straightened up and walked out from behind the carousel system, to find that a man had come unheard into the office while she had been filing.

The first thing she noticed was that his eyes were very blue, then as Elaine bustled forward to make the necessary introductions her heart sank.

'Oh, Dr Stafford, this is Danielle Roberts, our practice nurse. Danielle—Dr Stafford.' She looked from one to the other in a satisfied sort of way, then the smile died on her face as she couldn't fail to notice the tension in the office.

'It's all right, Elaine,' replied Dr Stafford tersely, 'Miss Roberts and I have already met.'

CHAPTER TWO

'SHE's already told me I drive much too fast for your country lanes,' Dr Stafford continued, while Elaine's jaw visibly dropped as she stared from one to the other.

There was an awkward little silence, then, without taking his eyes from Danielle, he said, 'You got your car home all right?'

She nodded, but before she had the chance to say anything he went on, 'I gather you've been on holiday?'

'Yes. . .'

'So when can we expect the pleasure of your company?'

She thought she detected a hint of sarcasm in his tone and she glanced sharply at him, but his expression was inscrutable.

'I shall be at work first thing in the morning,' she replied crisply. She was aware that the atmosphere almost crackled, then to her relief Dr Stafford glanced at his watch.

'I'm late,' he stated. 'I've been on a house call. Are there many waiting for me, Elaine?' He turned slightly to the receptionist, who seemed suddenly bemused by the events of the last few minutes.

'Oh—oh, yes,' she replied, pulling herself together

as he waited for her answer. 'There are four in the waiting-room.'

'I'd better get on, then—and while I think of it, Elaine, would you not book any late appointments for me tomorrow night? I have that meeting in the village hall at eight o'clock.' He nodded towards Danielle, 'The locals are thinking of getting up a petition to have your friends on the common moved on.'

'What do you mean,' Danielle's chin went up defiantly, 'my friends? I haven't seen them yet.'

'Really?' His blue eyes hardened. 'When I came in I thought I heard you defending them, and it certainly sounded as if you were on that boy's side this afternoon.'

'You mean, he's with them?'

Dr Stafford nodded, and Danielle knew then for sure that her suspicions had been correct, but before she had the chance to say more he gave a cool nod to them both and, taking a pile of patient records from Elaine, left the office, crossing the hall to his consulting-room.

As soon as his door shut behind him Elaine rounded on Danielle. 'Whatever was all that about?' she demanded. 'I didn't know you'd met him.'

'Neither did I,' replied Danielle cryptically. 'At least, I didn't know who he was.'

'But what happened?' Elaine was obviously not going to be easily put off.

'Oh, there was a stupid incident when I swerved to avoid a dog, that's all,' said Danielle, wondering how she could change the subject.

'But he said you accused him of driving too fast.' Elaine's eyes had widened in anticipation.

'Well, he was. He flew round the corner—these lanes just aren't built for speed like that, you never know what you're going to find round the next bend. In his case, it was me,' she added shortly.

Elaine grinned. 'So was he very angry?'

'Yes, I suppose he was. The boy with the dog got torn off a strip for not having it on a lead, and he bawled me out for leaving my car across the road while I went to see if the dog was all right.'

'And you had no idea who he was?' Elaine suddenly giggled.

'How could I?' protested Danielle. 'It was some way out of the village and he was travelling in the opposite direction—I thought he was someone just passing through. . .although,' she hesitated, 'I must admit, I got the impression that he knew the boy.'

'He probably did, if he was one of those hippies.' Elaine sniffed, then as a buzzer sounded she opened the communicating hatch to the waiting-room and called Dr Stafford's first patient, then, turning back to Danielle, she lowered her voice and asked, 'So what did you think of him?'

Danielle shrugged. 'What do you mean?'

'Well, did you think he was dishy?'

'Not particularly. I thought he was bad-tempered when I met him in the lane, and what I've seen since hasn't made me change my mind.'

'Maybe he has a reason for acting that way,' argued Elaine, then went on, 'but what I really meant was, do you find him attractive? That rugged outdoor look and those blue eyes. . .you have to admit, he's not the usual type we get around here—he looks more like an American film star than an English country doctor.'

'It's probably only the suntan. . .hasn't he been working abroad somewhere?'

'Mmm, Africa, I think. . .' said Elaine dreamily.

'Well, there you are, then—the African sun is enough to make anyone rugged; underneath he's probably pink and white and mottled like the rest of us.' Danielle laughed, then quite deliberately changed the subject, for there was no way that she wanted Elaine to even suspect that she had indeed been more than faintly disturbed by the new locum. He really was something quite different, obviously a hard man who, it seemed, might have lived a tough life, if his embittered demeanour was anything to go by, but it had been his physical appearance and the expression in his blue eyes when he had looked at her that had really shaken Danielle.

'So what's this petition about?' she asked swiftly, trying to put the disturbing images of Dr Stafford firmly out of her mind.

'It's these hippies,' explained Elaine. 'Some of the villagers are so fed up with them that they're getting up this petition.'

'And what do they intend doing with it?'

'I don't know really,' admitted Elaine. 'Hand it in to the police or the magistrate, I should imagine. . . anything just so that something is done and they get moved on.'

'Hmm, maybe I'll go to this meeting,' said Danielle thoughtfully, then, glancing up at the clock on the wall, she added, 'But right now I think I'll wander down to the common and see for myself just what all the fuss is about.'

Leaving Elaine to cope with a group of patients who had just arrived for the surgery, she slipped out of Westover. In the drive she passed an all too familiar red car, and she pulled a face as she thought of the way Dr Stafford had yelled at her that afternoon. She hadn't liked him at the time, and this second encounter hadn't been any friendlier. As she skirted the car and walked out into the lane she thought dismally that she hoped the situation would improve if she was to be working with him.

In the last few years the surgery catchment area had expanded further and further, and now included two other smaller villages and several farms and smallholdings deep in the Hampshire countryside. The responsibility for these areas usually fell to Dr Maitland, who held surgeries each week in the other villages and carried out any necessary house calls. Danielle always accompanied him and assisted at the surgeries, so she knew she would be required to do the same for Dr Stafford. Dr Griffiths, who was nearing retirement, only took surgeries at Westover now, leaving the outlying districts to his younger partner.

Outside the house Danielle paused and looked up and down the lane. It was quiet and there was no one else in sight. She knew she could go back to the village and approach the common across the green and through the woods, or she could walk on up the lane and backtrack to the piece of waste ground that the locals called the common.

In the end, because it was such a beautiful evening, she chose the former route, and as she entered the peaceful atmosphere of the woods she wasn't sorry. The bluebells were practically over now, but Danielle had seen them before she left for Devon and they had been particularly magnificent this year; a misty blue carpet through the smooth beeches and oaks that had stretched as far as the eye could see. Now the grassy paths were thick with pink and white campion and fresh green ferns were pushing through last year's dead bracken, uncurling their lacy fronds.

As she approached the common the birdsong, which until then had been the only sound in the silent woods, was joined by other sounds—a burst of distant laughter, the rattle of metal, the whining of a dog—and quite suddenly Danielle felt a tingle of excitement as she was transported back to her childhood in a moment of *déjà vu*. How many times in the past had she taken this very path after the whisper had gone round the village that the gypsies had arrived in the night, but in those days she'd had further to walk, for their encampment had always been on Farmer Jones's land beyond the common.

Now the sight that met her eyes as she stepped from the woods caused her breath to catch in her throat. At least a dozen caravans and wagons and one converted coach were drawn up in a semicircle on the common. Danielle narrowed her eyes. Was this simply a hippy convoy possibly on its way to Stonehenge for the summer solstice, or could there be any chance that some of her friends of so long ago had returned to Lower Yarrow?

It was many years since she had seen any of them—she had been about fifteen when they had last camped in the village, and since then she had heard that they had gone to Ireland to try their luck.

Several small children played on the grass between the caravans, and even as Danielle watched two men appeared from the direction of the village. They were both fairly young; one had a close-cropped haircut, while the other had his long hair tied into a pony-tail. They were shabbily dressed, and two dogs walked beside them, a greyhound and a lurcher similar to the one that Danielle had seen earlier. As they approached the coach, which had obviously been converted to living accommodation, the door opened and a young woman appeared. Danielle watched eagerly, but then felt a stab of disappointment, for they all appeared to be strangers. She stood almost hidden from view by the branches of a beech tree as the men disappeared into the coach and the woman called the children inside.

She sighed. She knew it had only been a very slim chance that any of her old friends had come back, but ever since she had seen the boy and his dog that afternoon she had had a very strong feeling that the gypsies had returned.

Suddenly she felt sorry for this group of travellers,

whoever they were, for it seemed as if they would shortly be moved on if the locals had their way. Her thoughts turned briefly to the meeting arranged the following evening for that very purpose, and she recalled Dr Stafford's look of irritation when he had mentioned it. It was all right for him, she thought angrily; he had fixed accommodation and no one would order him to move on.

She craned her neck to the far side of the common, where the lane and the roof of the house where he was staying were just visible between the caravans and the trees. The house, Foxworth, belonged to Dr Maitland. It was a lovely old stone Georgian-style building, but even Danielle was forced to admit that it really was very close to the common.

She was about to turn away when she suddenly heard a sound—a new sound, but a sound that touched a chord of memory. She paused and lifted her head and heard it again; the unmistakable strains of a fiddle. She turned her head and stared back at the common.

The sound appeared to be coming from one of two motorised caravans, which were parked a little apart from the others. She listened for a few more moments to be certain, then with a little cry of delight she began to run out of the woods, on to the common and through the parked vans, knowing now for sure that her instincts had been correct all along.

She only stopped when she reached the steps to the larger of the two vans, for by then it was perfectly obvious that that was where the music was coming from.

Feeling quite breathless, more from excitement than exertion, she lifted her hand to knock, but before her knuckles touched the door it was pulled open and a young woman stood in the doorway. She was about the same age as Danielle, with long black hair, sharp, knowing features and eyes so dark that they appeared to be almost black. She was also heavily pregnant. For a moment they simply stared at each other, then the girl gave a cry of recognition.

'Dani!' she cried. 'You are here—we couldn't find you. We thought you'd gone away. Look, look,' she cried over her shoulder to someone inside the caravan, 'Dani's here.' The sound of the fiddle stopped abruptly, and she turned quickly back to Danielle and gripped her hands, then, drawing her up the steps into the caravan, she hugged her fiercely.

'Maria—I hardly dared hope it was you,' cried Danielle as she returned the gypsy girl's embrace. 'It's been so long, so many years. I heard you'd gone to Ireland. . .' She trailed off as a tall figure suddenly appeared, and she found herself staring up into another swarthy face. 'Rollo,' she breathed.

A slow smile spread across the man's sharp features and he put down the fiddle he was carrying, then once again Danielle found herself in an embrace that almost squeezed the breath from her body.

'I only knew it was you when I heard the music,' she laughed. 'Only you could play a fiddle like that,

Rollo—you and Ezra. . .' She paused, looking from one to the other. 'Is Ezra here?'

Rollo shook his head and there was an awkward little silence. 'Ezra died two years ago,' he said quietly at last, as if it gave him pain to put it into words.

Danielle was shocked, for Rollo's brother hadn't been much older than him, but his next words brought the smile back to her lips. 'My mother's with us.'

'Sophia? She's here? Why, that's wonderful!'

'That's her caravan,' Maria nodded towards the other van, parked close to theirs. 'She shares it with Ezra's son Barnaby.'

'I must see her,' said Danielle. 'But first I want to hear all your news.'

Maria laughed and glanced down at her swollen stomach. 'This is my news,' she said.

Danielle glanced from one to the other of them, suddenly unsure of her ground, for in the old days these two had fought like cat and dog.

'Oh, yes, we married. . .in the end,' said Maria, sensing her uncertainty.

'And now you're to have a baby,' said Danielle, suddenly aware that Rollo was watching her closely.

Maria gave a short laugh. 'Oh, yes, a baby. . .to go with the other two!'

'The other two. . .?' Danielle gaped at her.

'Yes,' Maria put her hands on her hips and stared up at her husband, 'he doesn't believe in wasting time.'

Danielle glanced at Rollo and saw that a dull flush had touched his cheeks.

'So where are they? Your children?' she asked, glancing round the caravan with its brightly coloured furnishings.

'They're with Sophia,' replied Maria. 'I've been resting while Rollo went round the farms.'

'Farmer Jones has gone,' said Rollo.

Danielle nodded. 'Yes, several years ago now. Were you looking for work?' When he nodded she went on, 'There isn't any fruit-picking round here now, I'm afraid.'

'So we noticed,' he said drily. 'We haven't exactly been made welcome either.'

'I know,' said Danielle, and suddenly felt ashamed. 'I'm sorry.'

'It's not your fault,' he said calmly. 'Did you know they're trying to get us moved on?'

'Yes. I only got back today—I've been to see my parents in Devon—but yes, I've already heard that they're getting up a petition.'

Rollo shrugged. 'We're used to it. It happens all the time now.'

'There's to be a meeting tomorrow in the village hall about the petition. I'll go and try and put in a word for you.'

'You can try,' he said. 'But it won't do no good.'

'Well, I'll try anyway. I don't want you to go—it's years since I've seen you, and I want to catch up with everyone.'

'We're the only family left of the old band,' said

Rollo quietly, then when Danielle looked round in surprise at the other caravans he added, 'They're all travellers who've joined us in the last year or so.'

'Are there any Romanies?' asked Danielle.

'One or two say they have Romany blood, but we're the only ones who can claim to be true descendants,' he replied proudly, lifting his dark head so that Danielle caught the flash of the gold earring he wore. 'Come and see Sophia,' he said suddenly. 'She'll be pleased you've come. You were the first person she talked about when we stopped here.'

Sophia Lees was indeed pleased to see Danielle, welcoming her warmly into her caravan, the interior of which didn't appear to have changed at all in the last eight years. The bright colours, the reds, blues and greens of her curtains, cushions and furnishings were exactly as Danielle remembered them, and after she had admired the two sloe-eyed babies and Maria had taken them away to their beds she sat down on the comfortable old horsehair sofa.

Rollo sat on an upturned bucket in the corner, whittling at a piece of wood, while Sophia served herbal tea in dainty bone-china cups and Danielle admired the many silver-framed photographs of the family that covered every available surface. She was just thinking that it was as if someone had turned back the clock to when she was a teenager when Sophia set her cup down into its saucer and peered at her.

'So, little Dani, tell us about yourself. What has

been happening to you? Are you married? Do you have babies?'

Danielle was aware that Rollo had stopped whittling and appeared to be waiting for her reply. She threw him a brief glance, then with a laugh she too set her cup down. 'No, Sophia,' she said, 'no babies, and no, neither am I married.'

Sophia shook her head, and Danielle noticed that the thick hair drawn back from the darkly handsome features was almost without any trace of grey. 'You will be—you will, you see. You'll have babies too—Sophia knows these things. What of your grandmother, is she well?'

'She died two years ago,' replied Danielle.

'We too had great sorrow two years ago.' Sophia's eyes flickered to one of the silver-framed photographs, and when Danielle glanced up, Ezra's face smiled back at her. She was about to offer her sympathy, but Sophia gave her no chance. 'So what have you done with your life, if you have no man or babies to care for yet?'

'I'm a nurse,' said Danielle proudly.

'Ah. . .' The older woman nodded. 'You always had the gift of healing. . .you remember how you always wanted to help me when I mixed my potions and prepared my remedies? I always say. . .that girl is a natural healer.'

'Yes, Sophia, I remember,' replied Danielle. 'I loved to make tinctures and ointments and to watch when you applied them to cuts and bruises and made them better.'

'Do you work in a hospital?' asked Rollo suddenly from his seat in the corner.

Danielle shook her head. 'No, I work for Dr Griffiths in the village. . .' She paused as she saw the look that passed between mother and son. 'Is anything wrong?'

Sophia shrugged. 'Dr Griffiths is a good man. I remember him from before, but he has another doctor with him now.'

'You mean, Dr Maitland, his partner?'

'No, not him,' interrupted Rollo swiftly. 'The other one—Stafford, they call him.'

'Oh, yes, that's right,' said Danielle, her heart suddenly sinking. 'Dr Stafford is acting locum for Dr Maitland while he's away. Has there been any trouble?'

'He's staying over there, isn't he?' Rollo nodded in the direction of Dr Maitland's house, and when Danielle agreed he went on, 'He was none too pleased when he woke up one morning and found us camped on the common. We had a bit of a barney with him, and things have gone from bad to worse ever since.'

'Why, what's happened?' asked Danielle anxiously.

'Some of the younger children got into his garden and picked the flowers.'

'Well. . .I suppose that's only childlike,' began Danielle.

'And then sold them in the village. . .' Rollo concluded.

'Oh, dear, I see what you mean.'

'He wasn't too happy about that, and I think there

have been a few other things, then this afternoon Barnaby fell foul of him when his dog ran in front of Stafford's car.'

'Barnaby? That was Barnaby. . .Ezra's son?' Danielle looked up swiftly.

Rollo nodded, then frowned.

Danielle smiled. That explained why the boy had looked familiar. She had known him as a toddler, and he closely resembled his father. Briefly she told Rollo what had happened. 'So it rather looks as if we've all been victims of Dr Stafford's bad temper,' she concluded slowly, then added, 'And I have to work with him.'

'I think he could well be the one who could get us moved on,' said Rollo with a grim look at his mother.

Danielle stood up and, glancing at her watch, said, 'Well, that remains to be seen. I must get home now, but I promise, if I can do anything to help, I will.'

CHAPTER THREE

DANIELLE was at the surgery well before eight-thirty the following morning. She had changed into her crisp blue uniform and was arranging her appointments when Elaine arrived.

'Good heavens, you're keen after your holiday,' the older woman said as she hung her jacket on a hook behind the office door and picked up the jug from the coffee machine. 'What's the idea of getting here so early?'

'I wanted to be in touch with everything that's been happening,' said Danielle. 'Especially if I'm going to be working with Dr Stafford. I feel as if I got off to a really bad start with him, which doesn't make for a good working relationship.'

'You're both over at Pendleton this afternoon, aren't you?' said Elaine, pausing from spooning coffee into the filter to look over Danielle's shoulder at the appointment book.

Danielle nodded. Pendleton was one of the villages where the practice held regular surgeries. In the past she had always looked forward to these surgeries with Dr Maitland. Today, however, she found she was apprehensive. But first there were other matters to attend to—two morning clinics, one routine and one health-promotion clinic, which dealt with blood-pressure checks, diabetes and asthma monitoring, cholesterol and weight checks.

She was about to go through to her treatment-room beyond the office when Elaine suddenly looked up and said, 'Did you go over to the common last night?'

Danielle paused in the doorway and looked back. 'I did.'

'So what did you think?'

'I think there's a lot of fuss about nothing,' replied Danielle firmly.

'Did you know any of them?' asked Elaine curiously as the phone began ringing.

'As a matter of fact, I did. Only one family—the rest were strangers, but the Lees family were regular visitors to the village when I was growing up.'

'Are they aware of all the bad feeling towards them?' asked Elaine, stretching out her hand to answer the phone.

'Of course they are. It happens all the time,' said Danielle abruptly.

'Well, perhaps it would be for the best if they did move on, in that case,' said Elaine.

Danielle shook her head and would have carried on to the treatment-room, but once again Elaine called her back.

'I say,' she said eagerly, covering the mouthpiece of the receiver with one hand, 'his name's Nathan, by the way—did you know?'

'Who?' Danielle frowned, thinking Elaine was talking about a patient.

'Dr Stafford, of course. Who did you think I

meant?' Then, not waiting for her to reply, Elaine went on, 'I think that really suits him, don't you? Nathan Stafford. . .it sounds sort of strong and masterful. . .' She sighed, then, taking her hand from the mouthpiece, said, 'Good morning, Westover Surgery. Can I help you?'

Danielle found herself smiling as she began arranging her treatment-room, putting out fresh towels and checking her dressings. Elaine really was the most incurable romantic! Her life seemed to revolve around the soap operas she watched on the television and the dozens of romantic novels she read. Danielle didn't mind, just as long as she didn't try involving her in her schemes and fantasies, which she appeared to be doing now, with the arrival of Dr Stafford. She would have to be quite firm on that score, thought Danielle, and put Elaine straight right from the start. It would be just too humiliating if she said anything on those lines in Dr Stafford's hearing.

At that moment Dr Griffiths appeared in the treatment-room, and Danielle pushed all such thoughts firmly out of her mind.

'Danielle, welcome back,' he said. 'Did you have a good holiday?'

'I did, thank you, Dr Griffiths.'

'I trust your parents are well?'

'They are, and they send their kind regards.' She paused, then said impulsively, 'Oh, and last night I was talking to someone else who enquired after you.'

'Really? And who was that?' He looked interested.

'Sophia Lees.'

'Sophia? Good God, wherever did you see her?' He paused, then something must have clicked in his mind. 'Don't tell me she's with that hippy convoy on the common?'

Danielle nodded, but before she could explain Dr Griffiths went on, 'I didn't imagine any of the old gypsies were there. Didn't they go to Ireland?'

'Yes, for a while, but apparently Ezra died and they came back to this country. I don't think they're having much luck finding work, though.'

'Of course, they always came for the fruit picking, and that's gone now,' he mused, 'but old Sophia, she was a real character. Many's the argument we had over her remedies versus conventional medicine. Ah, here's Dr Stafford,' he said, looking up quickly as the front door opened. 'Nathan, have you met Danielle?'

'I have indeed,' replied Nathan Stafford, and Danielle felt her heart begin to thud uncomfortably.

This morning he was dressed in a safari-style shirt and trousers, which showed up his tan and sun-bleached hair more than ever. Danielle thought he probably hadn't had the time to go shopping since returning from the tropics and only had the clothes he had worn there.

He came right into the treatment-room and lifted his case on to the couch. 'I need to replenish my supplies,' he said, flicking open the locks and throwing back the lid.

'Of course.' Danielle unlocked her store cupboard. 'What would you like?'

As the locum helped himself from her neatly packed

shelves Dr Griffiths said, 'Pendleton today, Nathan; still, it should be easier than last week, as you'll have Danielle with you—she's worth her weight in gold.'

'Is she, indeed?' Nathan Stafford turned from the cupboard and looked at Danielle, who found herself squirming with embarrassment. She had always known that the older doctor had a soft spot for her, but she hoped he wasn't going to keep singing her praises in front of this man.

While Dr Griffiths ambled off to his consulting-room, calling to Elaine for his early-morning coffee as he went, Danielle tried to busy herself with sorting through the records of the patients she was to see that morning. This, however, proved impossible, for she was only conscious of the overwhelming presence of the man at her side.

As he was signing her record book for the drugs he had taken she found herself watching him. Once again she was struck by how tense he seemed, like a tightly coiled spring just waiting to snap, and she wondered what had happened to make him that way. She didn't for one moment imagine it could simply be the presence of the intruders camped on his doorstep that was causing this pent-up tension, although that probably didn't help.

Elaine had certainly been right about one thing, though. He really was extremely good-looking, in a hard, distant sort of way.

Almost as if he sensed her watching him, he suddenly straightened up, but the blue eyes were like chips of ice as he coolly regarded her. Danielle wondered what it would take to make him laugh.

'Right, Nurse Roberts, shall we get started?' he said crisply. 'My first patient is Mrs Dylan. Could you remove the dressings on her legs, then I'll come and have a look at her ulcers?'

'Yes, of course,' she said, then in an attempt to lighten the atmosphere she added, 'Shall I bring you in a coffee before you start?'

'I have my coffee at eleven o'clock—after surgery,' he said pointedly, then, snapping his case shut, he picked it up and walked from the room. She stared after him as he went, hating his aloof, formal manner. Things at the surgery had always been relaxed, and both Dr Griffiths and David Maitland were easygoing over everyday issues. It seemed now, however, that the atmosphere could be very different.

Danielle worked steadily, first with the ordinary morning surgery, then with the health-promotion clinic. Much of the time she found herself working with Dr Stafford, and by the end of the morning she grudgingly had to admit that his attitude to the patients was excellent. Maybe it's just nurses he doesn't like, she thought grimly—and gypsies, of course.

She was just attending to the last patient, a young girl who was attending the clinic in an attempt to get her asthma under better control. The girl had just used a peak flow meter when there came the sound of a commotion in the waiting-room. Danielle quickly recorded the reading on the girl's chart, told her that it was an improvement on the previous one, then went out to investigate.

A woman whom Danielle recognised as a comparative newcomer to the village was in the waiting-room with two young boys, one of whom had a towel wrapped round his hand. Elaine was trying to calm them down, as the boy with the towel was crying and the woman was verging on hysteria.

'It should be put down,' the woman shouted, 'same as they should. Vermin, that's what they are.' Then as she caught sight of Danielle she broke into a further tirade, from which Danielle concluded that the boy had been bitten by a dog, not a rat, as she had at first thought.

'Let's have a look at it, shall we?' she asked quietly, then, looking down into the boy's tear-stained face, she said, 'It's Jason, isn't it?'

He sniffed and nodded, and she put her hand on his shoulder and gently guided him to the treatment-room. She had recognised him from the periodic visits she made to the village school. His mother insisted on accompanying them, but Elaine persuaded the other boy to sit in the waiting-room and read some comics.

Carefully Danielle unwound the towel and saw that the bite was on the outer edge of the boy's right hand; several puncture marks in a reddened area that was already swelling.

While she was preparing antiseptic and dressings she said, 'Was it your own dog that bit you, Jason?'

'Of course it wasn't,' snorted the boy's mother. 'It

belongs to those damn hippies, that's what. I'm going to see that it gets put down—you see if I don't!'

A sudden movement in the doorway caused Danielle to look up, and she saw Dr Stafford standing there. It was quite obvious that he had heard every word. Trust him to be around when someone's running down the gypsies, thought Danielle angrily.

'Is everything all right, Nurse?' he asked.

'Yes, thank you, Dr Stafford,' she replied smoothly. 'Jason had a pre-school tetanus booster, and the actual bite isn't too bad.'

'What do you mean, not too bad?' interrupted the woman shrilly. 'Look at it. . .he could be scarred for life!'

Dr Stafford crouched down beside the boy and carefully examined his hand, instructing him to open and shut his fingers several times. When he was satisfied that all was as Danielle had said he stood up. 'Well, Jason, I think you'll live. Nurse Roberts will put a dressing on for you, and we'll take another look at your hand in a day or two.'

He was about to leave the treatment-room when he paused, and, looking at the boy's mother, he said, 'Did I hear you say it was one of the gypsies' dogs?'

'You did indeed,' she began indignantly, and would have carried on at greater length, but Jason suddenly chimed in,

'It was a lurcher, wasn't it, Mum?'

'Well, you said it was—I don't know one breed from another. But I don't really care what it was; it makes no difference; they shouldn't have dangerous dogs roaming around.'

'I told them to keep that dog on a lead yesterday,' remarked Dr Stafford. 'It nearly got itself run over, didn't it, Nurse Roberts?' Briefly his eyes met hers, and for the first time since she had met him she thought she detected a faint spark of humour. Then he was gone, back to his consulting-room, leaving her to dress the boy's wound. As she applied some sticky tape to hold the bandage in place she made an attempt to ask him what had happened.

'So how did the dog come to bite you?' she asked, quietly.

'It attacked him,' his mother replied sharply.

'So what were you doing at the time, Jason?'

He shrugged and began to kick his trainer against the leg of the chair. 'Nothin'. I wasn't doing nothin'.'

'So the dog just bounded up to you and bit your hand, is that right?'

The boy looked uncomfortable. 'Not really. . .we was playing, me and William. . .'

'William is your friend out there?' Danielle nodded towards the waiting-room.

'Yeah.'

'And what were you playing?' The question sounded casual enough, but Danielle was trying to prove a hunch she had.

'Just a game,' he put his head down, 'with sticks,' he added, then sniffed.

'So was the dog running around on its own?' Danielle persisted.

'Just what is all this, Nurse?' The boy's mother looked up indignantly, but Danielle ignored her.

'Was it, Jason? Was the dog running around?'

For a long while the boy remained perfectly still, his head down, then briefly he muttered, 'No, it were tied up.'

'Where was it tied up?'

He hesitated and shot his mother a frightened look. 'Behind one of them van things what they live in,' he mumbled at last.

'What were you doing down there?' demanded his mother. 'I told you not to go anywhere near the common and those scruffy unwashed louts, didn't I?'

'We was only playing.' Jason's voice took on a whining note.

'Were you baiting the dog?' asked Danielle. 'Poking at him with your sticks?' she added when she saw his blank look.

The boy remained silent.

'Well, were you?' demanded his mother.

He nodded.

'In that case, it's not surprising that the poor animal bit you, is it, Jason?' asked Danielle as she cleared away the dressing packets. 'In fact, I would say you were very lucky that it wasn't worse than it is. Maybe it would be a good thing to remember that most animals will lash out if they're being tormented.'

Jason and his mother didn't hang around for too long after that, and after Danielle had cleared up the treatment-room she saw that it was practically lunch-time. She usually went home for lunch, as her cottage was so close to the surgery. She went through to the office, where she found Dr Stafford checking his house calls with Elaine.

'I'm off now, Elaine,' she said quietly, hoping not to attract his attention, but at the sound of her voice he raised his head and looked enquiringly at her.

'I go home for lunch,' she explained.

'Really? He raised his eyebrows. 'Don't forget we're going to Pendleton. I shall want to leave at one-thirty.'

'I hadn't forgotten,' she said.

Elaine suddenly laughed. 'If you're worried about her being late, you needn't be—she only lives a stone's throw away, in one of those cottages on the green,' she added, then before Danielle or Nathan Stafford could say anything further, she said, 'Oh, Danielle, you won't forget my massage, will you?'

'No, Elaine, I won't forget.'

'Could you do it tonight?'

Danielle was suddenly conscious of Nathan Stafford's frown, and she desperately wished Elaine would shut up.

'No, not tonight, Elaine, I can't. I'm going to the meeting in the village hall.'

'Oh, I can't be bothered to go,' Elaine sighed.

'Does that mean you're not concerned about the gypsies parking on the common?' asked Dr Stafford.

'No, I suppose I'm not really. They aren't doing me any harm. Live and let live, that's what I say—besides, there's a good film on the telly later. So how about this massage, then, Danielle? What about tomorrow night?'

'I'll let you know,' replied Danielle, edging towards the door as she spoke, but before she finally made her escape she heard Elaine say.

'Actually, I think I'm a guinea-pig, really. I think Danielle wants to practise on me—she's into this aroma. . .aro. . .aromatherapy, you know. Maybe she'll give you a massage, Dr Stafford, if you ask her nicely.'

Danielle fled, not waiting to hear his reply.

She hurried across the green to her cottage, once again wishing that Elaine wasn't quite so forthcoming with other people's business. She hadn't intended telling Dr Stafford about her interest in aromatherapy, for, although the other two doctors knew and had no objections, she knew that some doctors didn't approve of alternative medicine. Probably because of the aggravation she had already had with the new locum, she could easily imagine that he would belong to the latter just to be awkward.

Now not only had Elaine blurted it out, but she had also implied that Danielle would give Nathan Stafford a massage if he so wished. Momentarily an image of him lying amost naked on a couch, waiting for her to administer the scented oils to his sun-bronzed back, came into her mind, and her heart began to pound. Then almost angrily she dismissed the thought—she was getting as bad as Elaine if she was going to start indulging in erotic daydreams about the new locum.

She had almost reached her cottage when she realised someone was waiting beneath the branches of Bessie's laburnum tree. This year the tree was so laden with the cascades waiting to burst into brilliant flower that it was difficult to see who it was standing by her gate. Then as she drew nearer Maria stepped forward to meet her. Danielle immediately noticed that she looked tense and worried.

'Maria, what are you doing here? Is there anything wrong?'

The gypsy girl frowned and nodded. 'I came to speak to you,' she said.

'Well, look, I'm just going to have a spot of lunch. 'Why don't you come in and join me?'

Maria hesitated and looked over her shoulder, and Danielle remembered that these people often found it difficult to enter the homes of others, almost as if they found it claustrophobic. She thought for a moment that Maria was going to refuse, then to her surprise she nodded abruptly, and when Danielle opened the gate she followed her up the path to the front door, which was almost hidden beneath a thick cluster of wisteria.

Inside she indicated for Maria to sit down, and while the gypsy girl sank thankfully down on to her sofa Danielle hurried into the kitchen and prepared some lettuce and tomato sandwiches and a pot of lemon tea. She carried these through to her sitting-room, placing them on a low coffee-table before sitting down opposite Maria and with a sigh of bliss kicking off her shoes.

'Oh, that's better,' she said. 'I don't think I've sat down once all morning.'

Maria didn't respond, and as Danielle passed her a plate of sandwiches she noticed that the worried look was back on her thin features.

'What is it, Maria? What's wrong?'

'You know Barnaby's dog bit that boy.' It was a statement rather than a question, and when Danielle nodded Maria went on, 'Barnaby thinks they'll put his dog down, so he's threatening to run away and take the dog with him.'

'Well, you can tell Barnaby from me that I don't think for one moment it'll come to that,' said Danielle, then, seeing Maria's doubtful expression, she went on, 'From what I can make out, it was all the boy's fault. The dog wasn't even loose, was he?'

Maria shook her head, then without disguising the bitterness in her voice she said, 'That won't make any difference if it's our word against theirs. You know that, Dani.'

'I know,' Danielle said quietly. 'But trust me, Maria. I'm pretty certain you won't hear any more about that incident.'

The girl sighed and leaned her head back against the shiny red velvet of the sofa, briefly closing her eyes. Danielle couldn't help but notice how tired and drawn she looked.

'When's the baby due, Maria?' she asked.

'Maria opened her eyes. 'In about three weeks.'

'And have you been keeping well?'

She shrugged. 'Not like with the others. I don't

want to be on the road when this baby's born. I'm so tired. All day I'm tired.'

'Would you come to the surgery?' asked Danielle, knowing full well what the answer would be.

'Sophia's looking after me. She'll deliver the baby just as she did the other two. She's been giving me wild spinach and the leaves of medicago and milk thistle. I don't know why I feel so different this time. . .' Maria sighed and trailed off.

Danielle set her plate down and leaned forward. 'Maria you're bound to feel tired; you've had two children very close together—how much difference is there between them?'

'Eleven months.'

'There you are, and now little Ezra is how old?'

'Fourteen months.' She said it dully, as if she had no fight left in her.

'Only fourteen months, and you're ready to have another—it's no wonder you're tired!'

'Rollo thinks it's the way of all women; he thinks I complain.'

'Well, I can assure you, it wouldn't be my way,' said Danielle fiercely. 'And I shall tell Rollo so when I see him.'

'Oh, no, you mustn't!' The gypsy girl's head shot up, and she looked more animated than she had the entire time she'd been in the cottage. 'Rollo mustn't know I've been here. He'd be angry if he knew I'd involved you in our troubles.'

Danielle sighed and sat back in her chair. 'The problem with you lot is your pride,' she said. 'You've always been the same. Even when you were children you wouldn't accept help from anyone—would you?'

The ghost of a smile flitted across the gypsy girl's features and a distant look came into her eyes, as if she too was recalling those far-off days when they had spent long, hot summers fruit picking, swimming in the river and sitting round a camp fire at night. Then suddenly another expression entered her eyes, one of pain, and once again Danielle anticipated what was to come. This time she braced herself for the girl's accusation.

'Rollo loved you when we were children,' Maria said, and although it was said without any trace of bitterness or jealousy there was still pain in her eyes.

Danielle leaned further forward and gripped Maria's hands. 'I know,' she said simply. 'I loved him too,' then as the girl raised her head and looked into her eyes, seemingly surprised by the unashamed admission, she went on, 'I loved you too, and Ezra and the others. I loved you all—you were so different from the other people I knew. I wanted to live my life like you, but it was impossible, Maria. I wasn't one of you.'

'Rollo would have liked you to have been. . .'

'Rollo was always meant for you,' said Danielle firmly, increasing her grip on the girl's thin brown fingers. 'Just as you were always meant for him. It was decided when you were barely out of your cradles you know that.'

Maria nodded, but there was still a sad little smile about her lips as she hauled herself to her feet. For a moment she stood looking down at her childhood friend, then she said, 'Our lives are so different, Dani; sometimes I envy you. . .' She broke off as the sound of the front door knocker filled the cottage.

Danielle jumped to her feet. 'Whoever's that?' She hurried through to the hall and pulled open the front door.

Nathan Stafford stood on the step.

Danielle's hand flew to her mouth in dismay while coolly he said, 'I thought I'd better come and collect you if we're to get to Pendleton in time for surgery.'

CHAPTER FOUR

WITH a little gasp Danielle looked at her watch and saw to her dismay that it was twenty-five minutes to two. She'd got so carried away with listening to Maria that she'd completely forgotten the time.

'I'm sorry, Dr Stafford, I'll be right with you,' she said, and, trying not to become flustered by his tight expression, she hurried back into the cottage to collect her bag.

Maria looked at her enquiringly. She must have heard what Dr Stafford had said, but instead of asking any awkward questions she simply said, 'I'll be going now, Dani. Thank you for lunch.'

'All right, Maria, I'll see you again soon—and don't worry,' said Danielle briskly as she followed her out of the cottage.

As she passed him Dr Stafford gave Maria a keen glance, but she kept her head down and didn't even acknowledge his presence. He turned and watched her walk across the green while Danielle locked her front door.

In silence he opened the passenger door for her, then took his own place in the car. He still seemed iritated, while she could have kicked herself for not keeping a closer watch on the time, especially after his earlier comments about setting out for Pendleton in good time.

The silence between them continued as he drove out of the village, then as they approached the main road he said casually, 'Can I take it that was one of the gypsy women you were entertaining to lunch?'

For a moment Danielle thought she detected a touch of sarcasm in his tone and she flung him a sharp glance, but his expression gave nothing away as he studied the road ahead.

'Yes, it was,' she replied briefly. She waited, expecting him to make some derisive remark about the gypsies in general, but instead he asked, 'When is her baby due?'

She threw him a curious glance. 'In about three weeks.'

'Is she having any medical attention?'

'If you mean is she booked into hospital and is she having regular antenatal checks from a midwife, the answer is no. But she's having the only type of medical attention she knows.'

He frowned, and as she glanced at him she noticed that this afternoon he wasn't wearing a tie and that he had undone the top couple of buttons of his shirt. A light tangle of sun-bronzed hair was just visible on his chest. Danielle felt her pulse begin to pound and she was forced to look quickly away.

'Is what you're saying that these people treat themselves?' he queried.

'I don't know about all of them, but the Lees family have always been treated by Sophia, who's the mother-in-law of Maria—the girl you saw at my cottage.'

'And does this Sophia have any formal medical training?'

'Good heavens, no. She uses all herbal treatments—ancient gypsy remedies that have been passed down through generations of Romanies. You'll never change them—they're convinced they know best.'

'I didn't think the girl looked particularly well,' he commented.

'She's very tired,' admitted Danielle. 'But then, anyone would be after three pregnancies in three years.'

'You sound as if you know her pretty well.' He looked curious now.

'I do—or, rather, I did,' explained Danielle. 'I hadn't seen the Lees family for a long time, about eight years, in fact, but when I was a child they came regularly to Lower Yarrow to work in the fields.'

'You've always lived in the village?'

'More or less—you sound surprised.'

'Yes, I suppose I am. I'm so used to travelling around that I find it incomprehensible that anyone wants to settle permanently in one place, and this is something of a backwater, you must admit.'

'I disagree,' replied Danielle, immediately on the defensive, as she always was if anyone criticised the village. 'It's beautiful here—I love it, I always have. In fact, I couldn't believe my luck when Dr Griffiths offered me a job.'

'I just thought it seemed rather quiet. . .'

'Then it's probably just as well you won't be here

for too long, isn't it?' she replied, feeling her anger beginning to rise. What was it about this man that everything they said to each other seemed to teeter on the edge of an argument?

They drove on in silence, but she was uncomfortably aware that he had seemed to find her brief outburst in some way amusing, for a tight little smile seemed to be hovering around his mouth. It was the closest she had seen him come to any form of humour, and she couldn't say she was particularly enthralled, for instead of making him appear more pleasant, as she had thought it might, it only seemed to give him a faintly derisive air.

They had almost reached the village of Pendleton when he suddenly said, 'Had she come to you because she was worried?'

'I beg your pardon?' Danielle looked bewildered for a moment.

'The gypsy girl—was she worried about her pregnancy?'

'I don't think so; only that she was feeling very tired.'

'She's probably anaemic—no doubt she hasn't had any iron tablets.'

'Probably not, but she has had wild spinach, medicago and milk thistle.'

'Good God!' He pulled a face. By this time they had pulled into the car park alongside the Portakabin that served as the village surgery. 'So if it wasn't her pregnancy, what was she worried about?'

Danielle had moved to get out of the car, but she

paused with one hand on the catch and turned to him. 'What do you mean?'

'Didn't I hear you tell her not to worry?'

For a moment she wanted to tell him to mind his own business, then she thought better of it. It wouldn't do to alienate him any further against the gypsies. At the present time they needed support, not antagonism. She took a deep breath. 'Maria was worried that there might be trouble,' she said quietly.

'What kind of trouble?'

'The kind of trouble that would result in them being moved on. It happens all the time,' she went on when he remained silent. 'You'd think they'd be used to it by now, wouldn't you? The eternal antagonism, the taunts, the gibes, the being blamed for everything that happens, but this time Maria was rather hoping they could have stayed in one place, at least long enough for her baby to be born. But that was before that stupid child got himself bitten by her nephew's dog. Oh, they're well used to that sort of thing—they know that's all it takes to have a whole village up in arms against them and to get an order to move them on.'

'I did warn them about keeping that animal under control.' He frowned again.

'That's the whole point—it *was* under control.' Danielle was aware that her voice had started to rise. 'In fact, it was tied up behind the caravans. Those dear children were baiting it with sticks, then they wondered why Jason got his hand bitten. If I'd been the dog I'd have bitten his arm off,' she ended angrily.

'I didn't know that,' began Dr Stafford slowly.

'No, that's the problem for these people,' said Danielle, getting out of the car and slamming the door behind her. 'No one ever knows all the facts—they just assume and jump to the wrong conclusions.' Then without waiting for him she marched angrily across the car park and up the steps to the surgery.

The atmosphere remained cool between them for the best part of the afternoon. A baby clinic had been arranged to follow the routine surgery, and as Danielle cleared her tiny treatment area after the last dressings, ear syringings and suture removals the first mothers and babies began arriving.

Dr Stafford was still involved with his last patient, so Danielle set up the baby scales and began counting out the various vaccines she would need. She was still feeling slightly on edge because of his attitude, and she found herself wishing that Dr Maitland was back. She had always in the past enjoyed the Pendleton surgeries; now she longed for this one to be over so that she could go home.

She wished she could define what it was about Nathan Stafford that upset her. She was sure it couldn't only be his disapproval of the gypsies, but she found it difficult to put into words. She only knew that she reacted strongly whenever he came near. She was still pondering the issue when the door of the consulting-room opened and the patient came out, followed by Dr Stafford.

'All ready for the babies, are we, Nurse?' he asked.

'Yes, just about. I'll put these leaflets out, then I'll call the first one.'

'You mean, we're not to stop for a cup of tea?' he asked.

Danielle looked up sharply, recalling his comments of that morning. 'I thought you'd rather wait until we've finished,' she said quickly, 'but I can get one now. . .' Then she saw the gleam of amusement in his blue eyes.

'It's all right, Nurse, I was only teasing. I'd rather wait until we've finished. It's just that since I've been at Westover I've never seen so much tea and coffee consumed in the course of a day.'

'Oh, that's Elaine,' said Danielle. 'I think she's addicted to caffeine.'

'Along with Dr Griffiths, I should imagine,' he observed drily.

'Well, you needn't include me in that. I only drink herbal tea,' she said briskly.

He raised his eyebrows and seemed about to say more, but at that moment one of the babies outside set up a tremendous wailing, and Danielle hurried forward to open the door and call the first patient.

By the end of the hour she had to admit that Dr Stafford had an excellent way with very young children. As he administered their vaccinations and gave advice to their anxious mothers on every topic from milk allergies to nappy rash, and chesty colds to weight gains, Danielle noticed a growing rapport between himself, the mothers and the children. She also noticed that the tension that had seemed so much to be a part of him had apparently eased. For the first time since that encounter in the lane the previous day he appeared relaxed, but she couldn't help but wonder how long it would last.

As she lifted the last baby off the scales and was recording the weight gain in her notes the mother mentioned that the child had a rash on her tummy.

'We'd better have a look, then,' said Dr Stafford, taking the baby from Danielle and gently removing her nappy. Carefully he examined the little girl and reassured the worried mother, then, turning his head, he said, 'I'll prescribe a cream for this and it should clear up in a day or two. If it doesn't, let me see Daisy again the next time we're in the village. Nurse, could you get me a prescription pad, please?'

Danielle hurried through to his room and picked up the pad from his desk, then as she stepped back into the treatment area she suddenly stopped. Daisy's mother had turned away and was sorting through the baby's clothing, but it was Nathan Stafford who commanded Danielle's attention.

He had lifted the baby from the examination couch; her head was resting in one of his strong-looking hands while the other hand supported the chubby little body. Her legs were kicking against his chest and she gurgled happily at all the attention she was receiving as she stared trustingly up into the face of the man who held her. And it was the expression on that face that had arrested Danielle, for as he gazed down at the child in his hands she witnessed a look of such tenderness, such compassion that she wondered if she was dreaming. Then, even as she watched, the look was gone, to be replaced by another, this time one of intense sadness, which, when he glanced up and saw her, quickly vanished.

The moment was gone. He returned the baby to her mother then wrote out the prescription, leaving Danielle wondering deeply over what she had just seen.

She was still wondering when they drove back to Lower Yarrow, and it was then that she realised that she knew absolutely nothing about the man at her side—only what Elaine had told her, and even that she had difficulty in remembering. She was sure Elaine had said he wasn't married, but there had been something about the way in which he had held that child that suggested that he had once been emotionally involved with another child. Had it been his own?

She threw him a sidelong glance, but his expression was set again and this time was giving nothing away. She had just plucked up sufficient courage to ask him something about what work he had done in the past when he spoke first.

'What's all this about you giving massage?' he said.

Danielle was taken aback by the suddenness of the question. 'Oh, yes,' she said, 'that's right, I do.'

'And aromatherapy, I gather. How did you get interested in that?'

'I've always been interested in plants and herbs and their healing properties,' she replied, uncertain from his tone whether he approved or not. 'I also happen to believe that if a patient's tension is removed and they can relax they're halfway to being cured of whatever ailment is afflicting them.'

'So is all this a throwback to your childhood association with the gypsies?' he asked, and this time she was sure there was a trace of scepticism in his voice.

'I don't know. It probably is.' She shrugged. 'But you needn't worry——' suddenly she was on the defensive '—I never let what I do interfere with my job. Both Dr Griffiths and Dr Maitland know about it, and neither of them disapproves—in fact, I think they recognise that it can be beneficial, and Dr Maitland especially is interested in many forms of alternative medicine.'

'It's quite all right, you don't have to justify anything,' he said coolly.

'I wasn't,' she retorted, then, biting her lip, she fell silent. They were at it again, arguing over the most trivial detail.

'So where did you learn to ease people's tension?' he asked as he drew the car to a halt in the drive of Westover.

'I attended a course in massage in Southampton,' she answered, trying hard to keep her voice steady, because she still had the feeling he disapproved. 'I've also studied aromatherapy through a correspondence course, then last week when I was in Devon I went to a two-day seminar on the study of essential oils and their benefits, but it's a vast subject and I still have a lot to learn.'

He unclipped his seatbelt and turned slightly towards her. 'Did I see a cat on your doorstep when I came to your cottage?'

Danielle nodded. 'Yes, you did. Why?'

He turned, opened the car door, and just before he climbed out he glanced over his shoulder at her. 'I was just thinking, only a few hundred years ago you'd probably have been burnt at the stake along with your friends on the common.'

'Yes, Dr Stafford,' she replied coolly, 'no doubt we would, by ignorant people who didn't know any better.' With that she too climbed out of the car and followed him to the front entrance.

'Talking of your friends,' he said as he opened the door and stood aside for her to precede him, 'can I assume you'll be at this meeting tonight?'

'You can,' she replied crisply. 'Someone has to speak up for them, and I'm pretty certain that someone won't be you.'

By the time she walked into Reception she could feel her anger simmering under the surface, and she felt badly in need of one of her own soothing techniques to reduce her tension.

'What's the matter, Danielle?' asked Elaine a few minutes later when she walked into Reception, shutting the door firmly behind her. 'You look hot and bothered.'

She didn't answer until she heard the click of Dr Stafford's consulting-room door. With a sigh she tossed her bag on to the desk and sank thankfully down on to a chair. 'It's him!' she said angrily. 'Honestly, he's absolutely impossible.'

'Whatever do you mean? What's wrong with him?' Elaine was staring at her in astonishment.

'I don't know—he's just infuriating. We argue all the time. . .if I say something, he says the opposite.'

'That could be a sign of attraction, you know,' mused Elaine thoughtfully. 'In all the books I read the hero and heroine don't like each other to start with, they fight all the time, then they——'

'Oh, don't talk rubbish!' snapped Danielle, then, catching sight of Elaine's pained expression, immediately wished she hadn't spoken so sharply. 'I'm sorry, Elaine, really I am—I didn't mean to snap. It's just that I've had a very trying day, and it isn't over yet—I've got this meeting to attend this evening.'

'Surely you don't have to go?' said Elaine.

'Yes, I do,' Danielle replied slowly, then she went on to tell Elaine about Maria. 'I'm sure all she wants is simply to be left in peace to have her baby in her own way,' she concluded.

'Somehow I very much doubt that will happen,' said Elaine drily, then, turning quickly from the desk, she said, 'Of course, you haven't heard the latest, have you?'

'Oh, no, not something else,' groaned Danielle. 'Go on, tell me the worst.'

'Apparently half the kids in the village school have got head-lice. Dr Griffiths has been writing prescriptions for Malathion all afternoon, the chemist has run out of all his stock, and you can guess who's getting the blame.'

'I don't see how they can blame the gypsies for that—their children don't even attend the village school, and they never have done.'

'Ah, maybe they didn't in your day, but they do now. Apparently they have to send their children to school in whichever area they happen to be, supposedly so that they can't be accused of depriving them of getting an education.'

'Even so,' Danielle shrugged, 'the head-lice probably didn't come from them.'

'You try telling that to some of those mothers who were in here this afternoon—I almost had a riot on my hands! Dr Griffiths had to come out and calm them down. No doubt they'll all be at this meeting, but as for getting up a petition, it sounded more as if they wanted to run the gypsies out of the village.' Elaine sniffed, then, dismissing the subject, she looked keenly at Danielle again. 'So what else have you found out about our handsome young doctor?'

'Nothing really,' admitted Danielle.

'Honestly, Danielle, you're the limit! I go to the trouble of fixing up a whole afternoon for you to spend alone with him and you tell me you haven't found out any more about him than we already knew.'

'I wasn't exactly alone with him, thank God.' Danielle rolled her eyes. 'We have seen one or two patients today, you know.'

'Oh, you know what I mean. Anyway, you were

with him in the car, weren't you? Didn't he tell you anything?'

'About what?' She sighed at Elaine's persistence.

'About himself. We know hardly anything about him.'

'That's not like you, Elaine; you must be slipping! He's been here—what? Nearly two weeks? I really would have thought you'd have found out something in that time.'

Danielle grinned and stood up, but Elaine seemed unaware of the teasing behind her comments. She stood thoughtfully chewing the inside of her lip, then said, 'I know, it's infuriating, but it really has been difficult. He's said virtually nothing about himself. All I know is that he's been working abroad and that he isn't married.'

'Actually, that's quite surprising,' said Danielle. 'He has a very good way with children—even more so than the average doctor. In fact, it wouldn't have surprised me to hear that he has children of his own.'

Elaine's eyes widened. 'Oh, do you think he has? Perhaps he's divorced and only sees his children occasionally.'

Danielle shrugged. 'I've no idea, but whatever his circumstances, he certainly isn't saying much about them.'

By the time she had left the surgery and was crossing the green to her cottage she had put all thoughts of Nathan Stafford firmly out of her mind and was concentrating on the meeting that evening in the village hall. She knew without any doubt that if she was going to speak up for the gypsies she would quite definitely be in the minority, but that didn't worry Danielle, for all her life if there had been any injustice to right or any cause to be fought she had always been known to plunge in headlong.

CHAPTER FIVE

THERE were more people in the village hall than Danielle had expected when she arrived just before seven-thirty. She sat fairly near the back and listened to the hubbub that was going on around her. The meeting had been arranged by the parish council, whose committee, under the chairmanship of retired bank manager Edward Pringle, were already in their places on the raised platform at one end of the hall.

As the chairman called for silence and outlined the reason for this emergency meeting, namely to discuss the presence of a group of travellers on the common, Danielle glanced around the hall to see who was present. As she had suspected, the majority were newcomers to the village. She would have been very surprised to find that it was long-standing residents of Lower Yarrow who were making such a fuss.

The audience appeared to have appointed a Mr Flint as their spokesman, a middle-aged, prosperous builder who had only recently bought a large house on the outskirts of the village. He was a short, stocky man with a florid complexion, and as he made his way to the front of the hall Danielle glanced round again. There was no sign of Nathan Stafford, but at the very back of the hall she glimpsed old Hilton Miles, who had worked for Farmer Jones and who had lived in the village longer than anyone could remember.

As Ralph Flint got into his stride he began listing the reasons why the hippies, as he called them, should be moved on.

'For a start, they're what I believe constitutes a public nuisance,' he said. 'They're noisy, disgustingly dirty and foul-mouthed, and we're convinced they represent a health threat. I believe, Mr Chairman, you'll find they're parked illegally, and it's the intention of this meeting to have them moved on.'

'Do you have an idea at the moment how you intend to carry this out?' asked Edward Pringle, staring over his half-moon glasses at Mr Flint.

'We do. We intend to compile a petition of signatures, a petition which we're confident will be signed by everyone in the village. We will then present this petition to the county council. I tell you, Mr Chairman, the villagers are sick and tired of this mob and will be only too glad to see the back of them.'

As he sat down there were cries of, 'Hear, hear,' some mutterings and a ripple of applause.

At that Danielle rose to her feet, and Mr Pringle turned his head to look at her. 'Did you wish to say something, Miss Roberts?'

'Yes, Mr Chairman, I most certainly do. Mr Flint is clearly under some misapprehension if he thinks he speaks for everyone in the village.' Her voice was loud and clear, and a hush descended on the gathering. 'I think you'll find there are many villagers who don't object to the presence of the gypsies on the common.

Those who are protesting seem to me to be people who've only recently moved to Lower Yarrow, people who don't understand our ways. Those of us who have lived here all our lives will remember that it was a yearly tradition for the gypsies to come here. They would stay for most of the summer, working in the fields, and as far as I can remember they never caused any more trouble than anyone else. It's true that their ways are different from ours—they have their own culture and customs, which sometimes seem strange to us—but they're peace-loving people if they're allowed to live without harassment.' She glanced round and noticed that there were one or two nods of assent, mainly from the more elderly members of the audience.

The chairman began fidgeting with his pen. It was fairly obvious that he hadn't expected any opposition and was surprised by what Danielle had said. 'Well, Miss Roberts,' he began, 'I can see the point you're trying to make, but the fact remains that this particular group of—er—gypsies doesn't appear to have exactly kept out of trouble. We seem to have had one complaint after another in the last few days.'

'Do you have a specific list of those complaints?' asked Danielle.

'We do.' He looked down at a bundle of papers on the table in front of him. 'There have been complaints of loud music and other noises late at night. There was an instance of children vandalising gardens and selling the flowers from those gardens. Dogs have been running wild in the village, and a local boy has apparently been badly bitten by one of these animals. A fight also broke out on the green between a gang of their youths and some of our youngsters. The presence of these dirty, scruffy individuals in our village shops is proving to be an embarrassment, and then today has come a complaint of a health hazard from mothers of children in the infants' school. I think you must agree, Miss Roberts, as a nurse, that this state of affairs just can't be allowed to continue.'

'Oh, I do agree, Mr Chairman. It can't be allowed to continue—it's about time we made a determined effort to understand these people, not hound them from place to place as if they were wild animals,' said Danielle firmly, then as a murmur ran round the hall she carried swiftly on, not giving anyone a chance to interrupt her. 'As to the complaints, I feel sure that if these incidents were investigated further you would find that, as with most arguments, there are two sides to each of them.'

'Can you be more specific, Miss Roberts?' Mr Pringle looked irritated now.

'I can. I feel sure that the noise that was mentioned was no greater than our own teenagers enjoying their weekly disco here in the village hall. The incident of the children and the flowers was regrettable and I'm sure will not be repeated.'

'What about the dogs?' someone shouted from the back of the hall.

'The gypsies were warned about keeping their animals under control, and I believe they've taken steps to make sure that they are.' Danielle turned as she spoke, and her heart jolted uncomfortably as she saw that Dr Stafford had come into the hall and was standing at the back. Fleetingly she wondered if he would join in the argument, and she braced herself to face his accusations.

'But one of them dogs bit young Jason,' said the same voice.

Danielle bit her lip. Because she had treated Jason, confidentiality forbade her to give any details.

'Yes,' said someone else, 'and you never know what diseases they're carrying. You'd think Nurse Roberts would be worried about that.'

'And then there are the nits—never had nits here before that filthy lot came.'

'What does Dr Stafford think about it?' said someone at the front of the hall, and several heads turned towards the new locum.

'You must be sick to death of them, Doc, parked on your doorstep,' called someone else.

'Yes, Dr Stafford, what are your views on this matter?' asked Mr Pringle with a note of relief in his voice, as if he was afraid that the meeting was about to get hopelessly out of control.

With a helpless little sigh Danielle sank back into her seat. Once Nathan Stafford had had his say she wouldn't stand a chance, she thought miserably.

Slowly he walked to the front of the hall, then turned to face the audience. 'I must admit,' he began in his low, steady voice, 'when I awoke one morning and found these people camped under my bedroom window I was less than pleased. I will also admit that there are certain aspects of their way of life that I find irritating, and over the past few days it's become increasingly obvious to me that many of you are very upset by their presence. As your local GP, albeit a temporary one, I'm more than concerned by anything that raises the stress levels of my patients, and this issue quite obviously is doing that.' He glanced round as he spoke, and when he realised he had the undivided attention of everyone in the hall he went on, 'That a solution must be found is perfectly plain, but, as Miss Roberts has pointed out, there are two sides to this issue. These are human beings we're dealing with, and they have their rights like everyone else.'

Danielle listened, hardly able to believe what she was hearing, then, just when she thought Nathan Stafford had had a complete change of heart, he said, 'However, I think there are a couple of issues that Miss Roberts has lost sight of. She talks as if all these people are the same Romany-type gypsies that she remembers from her childhood, but unfortunately that's not so. As far as I can make out, there's only one genuine Romany family in this group, while the rest is made up of travellers and hippies who may not quite adhere to the old Romany ways.'

'Too true!' shouted the heckler from the back of the hall.

'Move 'em on before there's any more trouble!' said someone else.

'I was going to add,' said Dr Stafford, raising his voice slightly, 'that I think some compromise could be attempted with these people.'

'Waste of time—they wouldn't know the meaning of the word!' shouted a young woman in the front row.

'The other point I want to make,' Nathan Stafford went on, 'is that, whereas in the past these people were able to find employment locally, I would imagine today they may find that difficult.'

'The one thing we're all forgetting is that they're parked illegally,' said Ralph Flint, struggling to his feet again and wiping his forehead with his handkerchief.

'But are they?' cried Danielle. 'Surely the common's for everyone?'

'Let the county council be the judge of that,' he replied. 'I propose we get this petition going, and the sooner the better.'

In the slight pause as he finished speaking, old Hilton suddenly spoke up from his seat at the back. 'Ain't no good goin' to council,' he said, and everyone turned to see who had spoken.

'Why's that, Hilton?' asked Mr Pringle.

'Council don't own common.'

A sudden hush fell on the hall, and Mr Pringle removed his glasses, while Danielle held her breath.

'If that's the case, Hilton, who does own the common?' the chairman asked.

'Of course the council owns it,' interrupted Mr Flint derisively. 'Who else would own it? It's common land—it must belong to the village, and we should have the right to say what happens on it.'

'I tell 'ee—council don't own it; never 'ave. It be private—the brigadier owns it,' said Hilton.

An interested murmur rippled round the hall. 'You mean Brigadier North up at Overton Hall?' asked Mr Pringle.

'Aye, that be 'im.'

'Well, in that case, the petition will just have to go to him,' replied Ralph Flint, and several of the audience nodded in agreement.

''Ave a job to.' Old Hilton chuckled. 'He's in India, one of them trekkin' 'olidays. By the time he comes back I reckons gypsies'll be gone anyway. I reckons you're jus' goin' to 'ave to put up with 'em.'

'No way!' Ralph Flint was on his feet again. 'There has to be a way round this, and I mean to find it.'

The meeting ended in uproar, with Ralph Flint stamping out of the hall in anger.

When Danielle stepped outside into the late-evening sunshine she found Nathan Stafford waiting for her.

'Interesting meeting,' he commented. 'Things aren't ever quite what they seem, are they?'

She shook her head, uncertain whether she should thank him for speaking up for the gypsies, then changing her mind when she remembered he had gone on to put a case against them.

'What will you do now?' He looked at her keenly.

'There's not much more I can do,' she said flatly. 'But I think I'll go down and see them and put them in the picture.'

'Mind if I join you?' he asked.

She hesitated, surprised by his request, then she gave a slight shrug. 'If you like.'

'I think it's time I met the Lees family and judged for myself.'

He fell into step beside her and they crossed the green. The grass had been cut that morning, and the slightly sweet smell of the newly mown hay filled the evening air.

'Why are people so prejudiced?' Danielle suddenly blurted out, unable to keep her feelings to herself any longer. 'Why can't they simply live and let live, as Elaine said this morning?'

'Prejudice usually comes from fear,' he said quietly.

'But what do they have to be afraid of, for heaven's sake?' she cried.

'Folk are afraid when they feel threatened, and they feel threatened when something is different from what they're used to—something they don't understand. There's always been an air of mystery about gypsies, superstitions tied up in their customs, and people have always been afraid of superstition.'

'But it's all so unfair. They aren't doing any harm.'

'Would they want to stay long if they can't find work in the area?' he asked as they left the green and took the path to the woods.

'I doubt it. But I got the impression that Maria just wants to stay until after her baby's born.'

'Maybe you should have said that in the meeting,' he mused.

'Do you really think it would have made any difference?' she asked bitterly. 'Besides, I have to be careful on that score, because Rollo doesn't know Maria came to see me. He's very proud and stubborn, and he'd be angry if he knew she'd discussed their private affairs outside the camp.'

'Rollo. . .is he the tall guy with the dark hair and the earring?'

Danielle nodded. 'Yes, that's Rollo, Maria's husband and Sophia's son.'

'I've seen him around the village.' said Nathan.

By this time they had entered the cool silence of the woods, their feet making no sound on the dusty leaf-mould as they wended their way through the fresh green ferns and the colourful mass of dandelions, campions and celandine.

As they walked in silence Danielle became increasingly aware of the presence of the man at her side. His sheer masculinity she found almost overpowering, to such an extent that she found herself searching for something to say to break the unusual tension between them. She was saved, however, when he spoke first.

'How quiet it is!' He paused a moment to look at the smooth beeches and gnarled oaks towering above them, their thickly clad branches a mass of motionless shades of green in the still air.

Danielle nodded and lifted her head, drinking in lungfuls of the sweetly scented air.

'I think I'm beginning to understand why you love this place,' he commented. 'I was brought up in Norfolk, wild flat country with endless skies and unbelievable sunsets—a place also of great beauty in its own way, but very different from this.'

'Didn't someone say you'd been working abroad?' Danielle stole a glance at him as they walked on. He was casually dressed that evening in a navy sweat-shirt and bleached denims, and while they had been walking he had seemed more relaxed than he had been since she had met him. This time it was she who felt tense and on edge. At her question, however, his features tightened again, and she instantly wished she hadn't mentioned his work. For a moment she thought he wasn't going to reply.

'I've been working in Africa,' he replied, confirming what Elaine had said.

'What part of Africa?'

By this time they had entered the slightly raised clearing on the edge of the woods, and the common stretched out before them. As if by mutual agreement, they stopped and gazed down at the circle of caravans, the small children who played on the grass and the few adults, some who gossiped on the steps of the vans, others who went about their work; taking in washing from an improvised clothes line, clearing rubbish or tinkering with one or other of their vehicles.

Once again Danielle thought Nathan wasn't going to answer her question, then as they moved forward he said, 'I spent a good deal of time in Ethiopia, but more recently I've been working in the Sudan.'

'And will you be going back there?' For some reason

she found herself holding her breath as she waited for his reply.

'Yes.' His reply was abrupt.

Danielle would have liked to go on and ask about the nature of his work, but his next words indicated that the subject was closed and that he didn't wish any further discussion. 'Which caravan is the Lees'?' he asked curiously, looking around.

'Those two over there.' Danielle pointed to the two caravans that stood a little apart from the others. 'They have modern homes now,' she explained, and there was a touch of regret in her tone. 'When I was a child they had the old-fashioned Romany caravans.'

They had to walk past the other caravans to reach Sophia's and Rollo's, and as they passed the other inhabitants they were aware of a sudden hush over the encampment and many suspicious glances.

'They don't trust us,' murmured Danielle, 'and who can blame them?'

'I shouldn't think I'm too popular,' he replied. 'Not after yelling at those children who pinched the Maitlands' flowers.'

The door to Sophia's caravan was wide open, and as they approached they could hear the sound of voices from inside.

'Carry on applying the tincture until the bruises are gone. The swelling will soon disappear and you'll be able to open your eye again.'

Danielle recognised Sophia's voice, then a tousle-headed youth appeared on the steps. One of his eyes was badly swollen and there was a deep purple bruise on his jaw. He muttered a reply to Sophia that might have been a thank-you, then with a furtive glance at Danielle and Dr Stafford he sidled away towards the other vans.

'Is there anyone else waiting?' called Sophia, and Danielle knew for sure then that the gypsy woman was holding one of her surgeries. She smiled, and, running lightly up the few steps, tapped on the open door. 'It's only me, Sophia,' she said, leaning forward into the van.

'Dani! Come in, come in.'

'I hope I'm not disturbing you.'

'You are always welcome, you know that.'

'I've brought someone to meet you.' She glanced over her shoulder as she spoke.

'Someone else for a remedy or a cure?' The gypsy woman had struggled to her feet and was trying to peer over Danielle's shoulder.

'Hardly.' Danielle was forced to smile. 'This is Dr Stafford—your neighbour,' she added as an afterthought.

'Ah, Dr Stafford. Come in—any friend of Danielle's is welcome here.' Sophia held out one wrinkled brown hand as he stepped up into her home.

'Mrs Lees, I'm pleased to meet you,' said Nathan, then added solemnly, 'especially as we're in the same line of business.'

It was the best thing he could have said, and Danielle smiled to herself in relief. She had been a little worried about the reaction on both sides from this meeting, but within moments they were talking as if they had known each other for years.

Sophia bustled about preparing her herbal tea, explaining as she did so that she had been busy in the last few days dealing with cuts and bruises after the late-night fight on the village green. 'Never mind, everyone's healing up nicely,' she said, then, peering up into Dr Stafford's face, she said, 'How about your patients? I expect you've had the other half to deal with.'

'Something like that.' He laughed, and Danielle glanced up quickly at the sound. As she had anticipated, when he smiled the hard lines of his features were transformed. The rigid jaw relaxed, the full finely shaped mouth parted to reveal strong white teeth and the blue eyes lost their icy stare.

Sophia, unaware of the transformation she had brought about, continued talking. 'As if all that weren't enough, today I've been preparing my special remedy of henbane for lice. We haven't needed that for years, but some of our children seem to have picked something up in the village school.'

Danielle didn't dare look at Dr Stafford, who appeared to be intently examining Sophia's collection of photographs.

'I hear you've had a meeting,' Sophia went on. 'How did it go?'

'That's what we've come to see you about,' said Danielle.

'Got to move on, have we?' Sophia said it in a

resigned way, as if she was well used to that sort of thing.

'Well, not immediately.' Danielle went on to explain about the common not belonging to the council. 'And apparently the owner's abroad in India, so they won't be able to approach him for some time.'

'The baby may be born by then,' mused Sophia, and Danielle threw her a sharp glance. Was she too worried about Maria's state of health?

Before she could ask, however, Dr Stafford intervened. 'Are you concerned about your daughter-in-law's pregnancy?'

The old woman shook her head and began passing round her bone-china cups of tea. 'No, she's a little tired, that's all,' her dark head lifted proudly, 'but there's nothing I can't cope with. It would be better, though, if she weren't on the move.' She fell silent for a moment, staring into her cup, then she said, 'Was there any other trouble?' She glanced at Danielle as she spoke, as if she knew that Danielle would know to what kind of trouble she was referring.

'There were all the usual accusations, Sophia,' replied Danielle bluntly. 'I did my best for you, but it seems as if some of the complaints were justified.'

Sophia muttered something about newcomers, and Danielle nodded and set her cup down. 'It seems as if newcomers are a problem on both sides,' she said. 'It's the new people to the village who are making the most fuss, because they weren't here when you used to come before. And I'd say it's the newcomers among your group that aren't keeping up your standards.'

'Bah!' Sophia made a dismissive gesture with her hand, as if she too was fed up with the behaviour of some of the later additions to the group.

'Maybe if your son was to have a word with them,' suggested Dr Stafford. 'Then perhaps if there weren't any more problems and the villagers can't get any further with their petition you may be able to stay here in peace, for the time being at least.'

As he was speaking a shadow fell across the open doorway and Sophia looked up. 'Here's my son now,' she said.

CHAPTER SIX

Rollo stood glowering at them from the open doorway, his hostile expression moving from Dr Stafford to Danielle and back to the doctor again.

'What's wrong?' he asked, and his tone was suspicious.

'It's all right, Rollo,' said Danielle quickly, remembering the look on his dark features from their childhood days and knowing that it used to precede a fit of temper, sulking or both. 'It rather looked as if there might have been trouble, but I hope we may be able to avert it, at least for a while.' She went on to explain about the meeting and what had happened.

'You'll have to have a word with some of the others,' said his mother firmly. 'They need to learn a few more rules of the road.'

'Huh, the only thing some of them are interested in is getting to Stonehenge for the solstice,' muttered Rollo. 'But I've told them even if they get anywhere near Salisbury Plain they'll only be moved on by the police.'

'Your best bet is to stay put for the time being,' said Nathan Stafford suddenly, then casually asked, 'Was that your wife I saw earlier—her baby's due very soon, isn't it?'

Rollo nodded, but the glance he gave Dr Stafford was still very suspicious.

'I think the best thing would be for you to remain here for as long as you can,' the doctor went on. 'I really don't think there's much the villagers can do now that we know the common is privately owned. If, however, they're able to contact the owner of the land and he wants you moved on, that will be a different matter. In the meantime I should lie low, and don't let the rest of your people make any trouble.'

'Thank you, Dr Stafford,' said Sophia, 'and thanks to you too, Dani.' She turned to the doctor. 'Dani has always cared about us, and do you know something? When she was only a little girl I knew she had the gift of healing.'

'Really?' As Dr Stafford raised his eyebrows Rollo adopted a surly expression, and Danielle fervently wished Sophia would shut up.

'Yes, she used to come and help me with my potions and remedies, so I wasn't surprised to hear she'd become a nurse. She should, of course, be married by now with babies of her own.' Sophia nodded her head wisely.

'You think so?' A note of amusement had crept into Nathan Stafford's tone, and Danielle, recognising it, squirmed with embarrassment.

'We really should be going, Sophia,' she said, standing up.

'You will come back to see us again?'

'Of course.' They took their leave of Sophia and the silent Rollo, and as they made their way back between the caravans Danielle was conscious of Rollo's eyes boring into her back, watching them from the foot of the caravan steps.

Dusk was beginning to fall and the path through the woods looked dark and slightly mysterious. 'I'll walk back with you,' said Dr Stafford.

'Oh, there's no need,' she replied quickly.

'No, really, I'd rather. I need the exercise, and, besides, it's getting dark.'

'That doesn't worry me. You forget, I'm well used to the woods.'

'Even so, I'd be happier if I knew you'd got home safely—you can't be too careful these days.'

'Do you mean I don't know who's about? Gypsies in the woods and all that?' she laughed.

'Actually, I wasn't necessarily thinking of your gypsy friends, although the black looks of the colourful Rollo could probably strike fear into any foolhardy late-night stroller in the woods.'

Danielle laughed. 'Oh, Rollo's all right—really, he wouldn't harm a fly.' She glanced at him. 'Thanks, by the way, for being so understanding back there.'

'You sound as if you were surprised, as if you didn't expect that I would be.'

'I was,' she admitted, then curiously she added, 'What did bring about your change of heart?'

He shrugged. 'Actually, I wasn't that much against them in the first place, believe it or not.'

'You certainly gave the impression that you were.'

'Did I? Yes, I suppose I must. But it was as I said—I was irritated by some of the incidents, the flowers in particular, probably because they weren't my flowers to pick, and because so many of the patients I saw seem to have been upset by the gypsies. But now, I must admit, you've made me see it from their point of view.'

By this time they had almost reached the edge of the woods, but as Danielle stepped from the path she felt a creeping bramble suddenly catch her foot. With a little cry she bent down to release it, only to find that it had entangled itself in the folds of her full skirt.

'What is it?' Nathan stopped and looked back, then, realising what had happened, he came back the few paces and bent down. 'Keep still,' he said and, taking hold of the bramble, set about disentangling it from her skirt.

Danielle stood still, suddenly acutely aware once again of his close proximity. She stared down in the half-light at the back of his head and his dark blond hair, which curled slightly where it met the neck of his sweat-shirt. For some reason the sight of that caused a delicious little tremor to travel the length of her spine, and when he straightened up, having discarded the offending bramble, she didn't immediately move. For a moment their eyes met, and it was as if the moment, with the silence of the woods around them, was suspended in time, then softly she said, 'Thank you, Dr Stafford.'

He didn't move; he carried on looking at her, then equally softly he said, 'I think it's time we dropped all this "doctor" nonsense if we're to be in each other's company for the best part of each day. My name's Nathan, and yours, I know, is Danielle.'

'Very well—Nathan,' she replied.

They walked on then in silence, but Danielle felt that they had got over the bad start they had made, and later that night as she prepared for bed she found herself going over the events of the past couple of days in her mind.

It really had been a most strange time, she thought as she opened her bedroom window and leaned out. The garden was bathed in soft moonlight, while the air was cool and fragrant from the many scents from her herb garden.

Seeing her gypsy friends had stirred all sorts of memories and deeply buried feelings, as had her conversation with Maria at lunchtime that day. It had come as no great surprise to her when Maria had talked of Rollo's feelings for her when they had been growing up. At the time she had been acutely aware of the passionate depths of the gypsy boy's emotions, while she herself had been trying to adjust to the changes in her own body as she had approached womanhood.

At one time she had even fancied herself in love with the handsome dark-eyed boy, but always she had been aware of Maria. She had known that Rollo and Maria had been promised to each other when they were babies and that neither of them would readily break the Romany betrothal.

When she was older and looked back on those magical summers of her childhood she had known there could never have been a chance of any sort of relationship between herself and Rollo Lees—they belonged to different worlds—but she had also known that in another time and another place anything might have been possible. And the events of the day had proved to her that Rollo was well aware of that too. She knew that behind the suspicious look he had given Nathan Stafford there simmered a measure of jealousy, and she wondered fleetingly if Nathan had recognised it.

But why should Rollo have been jealous of the new doctor? Was it merely because she was working with him and that for the next couple of weeks at least she would be spending the best part of every day at his side—or was there another reason?

Rollo, being Romany, was very perceptive, and like his mother he often saw situations that hadn't yet happened, or tuned in to vibrations between people. And, Danielle was forced to admit, there was certainly some sort of hidden tension between herself and the new locum. It had started as irritation with each other, anger even, but now that had been practically resolved, and still there remained a tension between them, which she found difficult to explain. That Nathan Stafford was aware of it, too, she was pretty certain, for it had been at its strongest that evening in the woods when they had faced each other and neither had been able to look away.

At that moment a cloud crossed the moon, blotting out the light. Danielle shivered slightly and withdrew into the bedroom, shutting the window. There had also been his reluctance to talk about his work and that air of pent-up anger about him that had so intrigued her. At first she had been convinced that his anger had been directed at her, but now she was certain there was something else that was eating away at him.

She turned back the sheets, delicately scented with her own perfumed oils, then climbed into bed. Her last thought before sleep claimed her was that maybe the following day she would find out more about Nathan Stafford.

The next few days, however, proved to be so hectic that Danielle had little time to even talk to the new locum unless it was about their patients. And if he had been aware of any change in their relationship he certainly gave no indication of it. By the end of the week Danielle found herself wondering if she had dreamt their visit to the gypsy camp and the walk through the woods that had followed.

Part of the reason for their increased workload was the fact that Elaine had been away from work for a few days with a stiff back. She often suffered with back trouble, for which she had tried various treatments, ranging from bed-rest to physiotherapy and pain-killers.

When she returnted to work she once again suggested that Danielle gave her a massage. 'I've had a word with Dr Griffiths about it,' she said, 'and he says it may not work a miracle cure, but it certainly won't do any harm.'

'Very well, come to the cottage this evening and I'll see what I can do,' said Danielle, then, glancing at the clock on the office wall, she said, 'I must fly—

we're at Pendleton again this afternoon, and you know what a stickler for punctuality Nathan is.'

'Oh, so it's "Nathan" now, is it?' Elaine's eyes widened knowingly.

'His idea, not mine,' said Danielle hurriedly.

'How have you been getting on with him?'

'Oh, not too badly.'

'He still seems very uptight about something.'

'So you've noticed that as well.'

Elaine sighed. 'It must be another woman.'

'Not necessarily,' replied Danielle quickly—too quickly—and Elaine picked up on it immediately.

'Touchy on that subject, are we?'

'Of course not!' Danielle laughed. 'Don't be silly—what's it to me whether there's another woman or not?'

'What indeed?' said Elaine, and turned to answer the phone.

Danielle hurried from the office, trying to dismiss the ridiculous conversation she had just had with Elaine but for some reason found she couldn't. Although she had denied any interest in whether or not Nathan Stafford was involved with anyone else, she knew that deep down she really wanted to know.

In the hall she almost collided with Nathan as he came out of his consulting-room.

'Ah, all ready, Danielle?' he asked. 'Good, we're in plenty of time.'

They took their seats in his car, and as they drove through the village they passed two women with their young children who were obviously from the common.

'All seems quiet there for the moment,' observed Nathan. 'Have you seen anything of them in the last few days?'

Danielle shook her head. 'No, I've been too busy, but I did hear in the village shop that Ralph Flint has still gone ahead with his petition.'

'What does he intend doing with it?'

'Goodness knows—perhaps he's going to send it to the brigadier in India.'

They laughed and carried on to their afternoon surgery, but only a couple of hours later the name of Flint came up again.

Danielle took a call from Elaine, who said that an emergency call had come into the surgery and that Dr Griffiths was already out on another visit.

'OK, Elaine,' said Danielle. 'Give me the details, I'll pass them on to Dr Stafford.'

'It's a call from Bagwich Stables. Apparently Melanie Flint, Ralph Flint's daughter, has been thrown from a horse. They want a doctor up there right away.'

Minutes later they had locked the Pendleton surgery and were on their way through the steep narrow lanes towards Bagwich.

The stables formed part of a large farm owned by a family called Herrington. It was situated high on a crest of land overlooking the villages in the valley below, and was reached by a single cart track that bumped for a couple of miles over rough land.

'I'm beginning to see why the other doctors have Land Rovers,' said Nathan ruefully as he changed gear.

Danielle smiled. 'Yes, some of the visits are a little far-flung, but I think David Maitland quite enjoys his trips away from the surgery.'

'Oh, I do too. It was only the car tyres I was concerned about, not the distance. After all, I'm used to driving rather longer distances than from Pendleton to Bagwich.'

'Yes, I suppose you are,' she replied, hoping that he was going to enlarge on that statement.

She wasn't disappointed this time, for he carried on almost as if he hadn't thought about what he was saying.

'It was nothing for me to drive five hundred miles across the desert from one medical station to another. And that in temperatures of well over a hundred degrees,' he added.

'Was the country beautiful?' She stole a glance at him, pleased that at last he had mentioned Africa instead of changing the subject, as he had done on every other occasion when his work had been mentioned.

'Beautiful?' He frowned. 'Not in the way you'd think of as beautiful. But yes, I suppose it has a beauty of its own. It's wild, dramatic country, cruel, driving people to their limits, but certainly not beautiful in the way you would define it. Not, for example, like that.' They had reached the top of the crest and he had pulled into a gateway so that they could see right down into the valley below. Then, pulling forward again, they turned a bend in the track and the farm and stables were stretched out before them.

There seemed to be quite a bit of activity in the stable yard as they drew in. Several horses were saddled and a group of youngsters appeared to be about to embark on a lesson. One groom was washing down the yard with a stiff broom, while another was grooming a large chestnut-coloured mare. Other horses looked enquiringly over the open tops of their stable doors, and as Danielle and Nathan climbed from the car a tall fair-haired woman in her forties, dressed in jodhpurs and a hacking jacket, came out of the tackroom and walked across the yard towards them.

'Hello, Danielle,' she said. 'Thank you for coming so promptly.' She turned enquiringly to Nathan.

'Jennifer, this is Dr Stafford,' Danielle introduced, then, turning to Nathan, said, 'This is Jennifer Herrington. She and her husband own the farm and the stables.'

They shook hands, then Nathan said, 'Where's the patient?'

'She's in the farmhouse. I know you're going to say she shouldn't have been moved, but I'm afraid she got up off the ground of her own accord and came into the house.' They fell into step beside Jennifer and began to walk across the yard towards an archway on the far side.

'Are there any obvious injuries?' asked Nathan.

'She said she bumped her head. She was awfully pale and she seemed a bit sleepy. We haven't let her go to sleep, but I thought it best to get her checked over—we can't afford to take any chances.' She pulled a face at Danielle as she spoke, and Danielle got the feeling that she meant that they couldn't take any chances with the daughter of a man like Ralph Flint.

'Was she wearing a hat?' asked Nathan as they walked under the archway and along a path at the side of the large grey stone farmhouse.

'Apparently not,' replied Jennifer Herrington grimly.

'But I seem to remember that's one of your strictest rules up here,' said Danielle.

'It is. But unfortunately Melanie Flint's a law unto herself. She has her own pony, which we stable here, so she more or less comes and goes as she pleases and it's difficult to keep tabs on her as we do on the children who come for lessons. Today, apparently, according to my groom, Melanie arrived with a boy and she was showing off, trying to impress him, no doubt, when her pony, Boy Blue, must have had enough and decided to chuck her off.' Jennifer said it in such a way as if she didn't blame the pony, and Danielle smiled as they followed her into the farmhouse.

They found Melanie Flint lying on a couch in the study, and she did indeed look very pale. Her long dark hair was spread out over the cushions and a large bump had appeared on her right temple. She looked sulky, and barely acknowledged Dr Stafford. When Danielle saw that there was nothing for her to do she stood back while the doctor carefully examined the girl.

'Well, there aren't any bones broken,' he said when

he had finished, and Jennifer gave an audible sigh of relief. 'But I'd like you to have an X-ray to make sure nothing's happened under that bump.' He sat down and wrote out an X-ray request form. 'You'll have to go to the casualty department at the hospital. Now, I don't think we need call an ambulance for that. Do you have anyone who can take you?' He glanced up at Jennifer Herrington as he spoke.

She nodded. 'I've phoned Melanie's father,' she said. 'He's on his way here now.'

Nathan straightened up. 'Well, in that case, there's little else I can do.' He looked down at Melanie as he spoke. 'You're very privileged to have your own pony, Melanie. It's quite a responsibility for someone so young.'

'I'm nearly sixteen!' she retaliated.

'Really? I would have thought someone of that age would have shown enough responsibility to always wear a hard hat.'

A contemptuous look came into the girl's dark eyes. 'Hard hats went out with the Ark,' she said haughtily. 'Helmets are in these days.'

Nathan shrugged. 'Whatever—hat or helmet, it makes no difference to me, but it could make a great deal of difference to you. Now make sure you get plenty of rest in the next few days.'

He followed Danielle out of the study, and as they stepped outside again he murmured, 'Like father, like daughter.'

She smiled grimly and nodded, then Jennifer turned and said, 'Thank you so much, Dr Stafford. I do appreciate your coming. Do you need to wait and see her father?'

'I don't think that will be necessary,' he said firmly, and Danielle smiled. By this time they had walked back into the stable yard, and Nathan stopped and looked around.

'Do you have horses for hire?' he asked.

'We do organised hacks every day,' replied Jennifer, 'but yes, we do hire out horses by the hour—talking of which,' she turned to Danielle, who had stepped towards one of the stables and was smoothing the velvety nose of a sad-eyed grey, 'we haven't seen you up here lately, Danielle.'

'I've been away for a couple of weeks,' she replied 'and before that I was pretty busy, what with one thing and another. But yes, I was just thinking I'd like to book a ride.'

'When did you have in mind?'

'How about Sunday afternoon?'

'Could you include me on that?' asked Nathan, and both women turned to look at him.

'I'm sorry,' Jennifer hesitated, 'but I have to ask—are you an experienced rider? Otherwise, I'm afraid you'll have to join one of the organised hacks.'

He smiled. 'Is riding to hounds in a Norfolk hunt experience enough?'

'Oh, gosh, yes, I should say so!' Jennifer laughed. 'Sorry, but we have to make sure. Now, which horses would you like, Danielle?'

Danielle, however, was staring at Nathan in amazement and didn't hear Jennifer's question until she had asked it for the second time.

'Oh, sorry.' She hesitated. 'Could I ride Poppy?'

Jennifer nodded, and standing back a pace, she shrewdly looked Nathan up and down. 'Of course you can, and I'd think Sultan would suit the doctor, wouldn't you?'

CHAPTER SEVEN

'Do you think Melanie will be all right?' Danielle asked as they drove away from Bagwich.

Nathan nodded. 'Yes, I'm pretty sure she will, just a touch of mild concussion, but the X-ray will make absolutely certain—as much for Jennifer Herrington's peace of mind as anything. I can imagine Flint bringing all sorts of charges against the stables if anything happened to his daughter, whether it was their fault or not.'

'Yes,' Danielle agreed. 'He's that type of man.' Then she looked curiously at the man at her side. 'I didn't know you enjoyed horse-riding.'

A smile touched his mouth. 'I expect there are a lot of things about me you don't know.'

'Yes. I dare say there are.' She did nothing to hide the cryptic note in her voice.

'I could say the same about you.' Briefly he took his eyes from the lane ahead and gave her a speculative look. 'I didn't somehow put you as the sporty type.'

'Oh, I'm not,' she said quickly in case he got the wrong impression. 'Horse-riding is really the only sport I enjoy. I've ridden since I was a child.'

'Same with me.' He nodded. 'My father was master of the hunt, so I suppose it was inevitable that I should follow in his footsteps.' When Danielle remained silent he threw her another glance. 'Do I detect a hint of disapproval over riding to hounds?' he asked.

'You most certainly do,' she replied firmly. 'Oh, I don't doubt you'll trot out all the usual old clichés about keeping the foxes under control for the farmers, et cetera, but you won't make me change my mind. I don't like blood sports and I never shall.'

'I wouldn't dream of trying to change your mind,' he said mildly. 'To me it was a way of life, I was brought up to it, although it's a very long time now since I've ridden to hounds. But I guessed it wouldn't be your scene.'

'You did?' Danielle looked faintly surprised.

'Yes, and I dare say you're a vegetarian as well, am I right?'

'Well, yes, I am, as a matter of fact,' she admitted. Suddenly she felt embarrassed: was she really that transparent?

'Anyway, it doesn't really matter, does it?' He smiled, and once again she was amazed at how it transformed his features. 'I shouldn't for one moment think there'll be any foxes around on Sunday, and if there are I promise I won't chase them.'

By this time they had reached Lower Yarrow. 'Do you want me to drop you off at the cottage, or are you coming back to the surgery?' he asked as they drove through the village.

'Oh, the cottage, please. I have Elaine coming

round shortly,' she said after glancing at her watch, 'for her massage,' she added.

'I shall probably need a massage after our ride on Sunday. It's a long time since I've ridden a horse—I shall probably find muscles I didn't know I had!'

Once again the image of her administering a massage to Nathan Stafford slipped unbidden into Danielle's mind, and as she stepped out of the car she suddenly felt hot with confusion.

She stood for a moment outside the cottage and watched him drive away. Then with a little sigh she turned and walked inside. She was forced to admit that Nathan really was turning out to be very different from what she had imagined when they had first met. At times there was still that tension about him, and she had yet to find out the cause of that. Elaine had said it was probably caused by a woman, and, whereas at the time Danielle had been inclined to agree with her, she now found herself hoping that it wasn't.

Then as she went into her kitchen to feed Shelley she gave herself a little shake. What did it matter to her whether or not Nathan Stafford had a woman in his life? Really, she was getting as bad as Elaine! she scolded herself.

Elaine arrived shortly after six, and Danielle took her upstairs to her second bedroom, which she had converted into an attractive little treatment-room with a couch, a Chinese printed screen and a cabinet, which held the rows of phials of essential oils that she used for her aromatherapy. She had earlier added to a bowl of warm water a few drops of a perfume that she had especially created from lemon, bergamot, mandarin and rosewood. It gave the room a refreshing citrus aroma that Elaine commented on as soon as she stepped inside.

While Elaine undressed, Danielle washed her hands, then began mixing the oils she wanted to use. Because Elaine had been suffering from backache she added ten drops of rosemary oil, ten drops of marjoram and ten drops of sage to thirty millilitres of sesame oil.

'I hope this is going to do some good,' commented Elaine as she climbed on to the couch. 'My back's been really stiff again today, and I've got my stall to organise tomorrow at the fête.'

'I'd almost forgotten the fête,' said Danielle as she poured a little of the oils into the palm of her hand, then gently rubbed her hands together. 'There's been so much going on just lately that I don't seem to have had much time.'

'Well, if you're feeling guilty you can give me a hand on my bookstall,' said Elaine, then she sighed as Danielle began her massage, starting in the lower lumbar region of her back, then sliding her hands up on either side of her spine before bringing them down on the outer edges.

'I wasn't exactly feeling guilty,' Danielle laughed, 'but I'll certainly give you a hand.'

'Did you know they'd asked Dr Stafford to open the fête?' asked Elaine.

Danielle paused fractionally in the rhythmic movement. 'Have they? He didn't say.'

'He's not a great conversationalist, is he?'

'Well, he wasn't at first, I agree, but he's opened up a bit more in the last day or so.'

'Really?' Immediately Elaine was agog to know more, and Danielle wished she hadn't said anything. 'In what way?' she persisted

'Well, I found out he likes horse-riding.'

'Does he, now? I say, Danielle, you'll have to take him up to Bagwich with you next time you go.'

Danielle hesitated but didn't falter in the strong but gentle movements of the massage. 'It's funny you should say that. . .'

'You mean you've already arranged it?' Elaine moved in her excitement and tried to twist her head to look at Danielle.

'You must keep still, Elaine.'

'Sorry. . .but seriously, is he going with you?'

'Yes, on Sunday,' admitted Danielle. 'It was arranged when we went on that call up at the stables.'

'Oh, I say, I can foresee a romance here!' said Elaine excitedly.

'Will you stop talking such rubbish? You're meant to be relaxing,' scolded Danielle.

Elaine fell silent after that and Danielle tried to concentrate on the massage but now that thoughts of Nathan had entered her mind again she found it difficult to dismiss them. Was there any truth in what Elaine was implying? Was she becoming interested in their intriguing locum? Of course she wasn't, she told herself firmly, but as the heady aroma of the oils filled her senses she knew that deep down she was looking forward to Sunday.

'Oh, Danielle, that's absolutely marvellous,' murmured Elaine a little later. 'I've never felt so relaxed.'

'Well, if you find it's been beneficial you can come back for another,' said Danielle as she brought the massage to an end.

The summer fête at Lower Yarrow was always held on the village green on a Saturday early in June. It was organised by the parish council, who set up separate committees for each of the activities involved. The ladies of the Women's Institute ran the cake stall and were responsible for refreshments. The members of the sewing circle were in charge of the handicraft stalls, the children from the local school gave displays of country dancing, and the vicar organised afternoon sports for the children. It had always been the custom that anyone who lived in the village and had anything handmade to sell was permitted to set up a stall, later giving a percentage of their profits to the parish council funds. In the past this arrangement had worked well.

This year, however, as Danielle made her way across the green early on Saturday morning to help Elaine with her bookstall she could see that there were going to be problems.

For a start, the spell of fine weather they had been enjoying looked as if it might be in danger of coming to an end. The sky was grey and overcast, and a keen breeze whipped round the little groups trying to erect their stalls. Already yards of bunting had blown across the grass, and two of the Women's Institute ladies were chasing a couple of paper tablecloths that had taken flight and wrapped themselves around the trunk of a horse-chestnut tree.

But the weather wasn't the only potential source of trouble, and Danielle's heart sank as she realised that a heated argument was going on at one corner of the green.

Instinctively she guessed what was happening even before she saw Rollo's tall figure, for in the past the gypsies had set up their own stall at the village fête.

When she reached the group she found the vicar trying to defuse the row, which was between Rollo and Ralph Flint. Immediately she saw what the problem was. Ralph Flint was setting up a stall for his wife that consisted of dried-flower arrangements and carved wooden models. He insisted these had all been made by members of his family, but Danielle strongly suspected he'd bought in the merchandise to be sold.

The gypsies' stall was similar, with its carvings, dried flowers, herbs and grasses, but there the similarity ended, for everything on their stall was from a natural source and had been hand-crafted by themselves.

'I've suggested that Mr Flint moves his stall to the other side of the green,' said the vicar with a worried frown, 'but he won't hear of it. He says the gypsies have no right to be here anyway. The trouble is, the gypsies were here first. They apparently set up their stall at about six o'clock this morning.'

'Yes,' said Danielle, 'they would.'

At that moment Mr Pringle, the chairman of the parish council, caught sight of her and detached himself from the group. 'Do you think you could have a word with these people, Miss Roberts? You do seem to have some influence with them.'

'What do you want me to do?' asked Danielle patiently. 'I can hardly ask them to go away. At the present moment they're resident in the parish, and the rules of the fête clearly state that anyone who's a resident has the right to set up a stall.'

'I know, I know,' said Mr Pringle, his agitation clearly showing. 'But perhaps you could ask them to move to the other end of the green, well away from the Flints. Oh, dear,' he glanced anxiously at the darkening sky, 'was that a spot of rain I felt?'

Danielle moved across to the group of gypsies who were grouped around their stall. Barnaby was with Rollo, and there were half a dozen women from their group, dressed in their long flowing muslin clothes with flowers plaited into their hair. There was no sign of Sophia or Maria.

Rollo looked up as she approached and she saw he had a stubborn, mulish look on his face.

'Hello, Rollo,' she said quietly.

He nodded and his expression softened slightly as he stared down at her. 'I suppose you're going to tell us to go now,' he said bitterly.

'No, Rollo, I'm not. You've as much right to be

here as anyone else, but what I am going to suggest is that you move your stall to the other side of the green—out of harm's way,' she added, her glance flickering to Ralph Flint.

'We were here first. . .' growled Rollo, and several of his group nodded in agreement.

'I know. . .I know you were,' said Danielle gently. 'Just as I know that what you're selling is the genuine thing, but I really think that in the circumstances it would be better if you were to move.'

He stared down at her for a long moment and she found it difficult to read the expression in his dark eyes, then he shrugged. 'All right,' he muttered. 'But only because you've asked, Dani. That's the only reason.'

She gave a sigh of relief as he instructed his group to dismantle their stall and move their wares.

The threatened shower came just before midday, and eveyone scurried around, covering the stalls and sideshows with sheets of polythene. Then for the next half-hour everyone, gypsies and villagers alike, huddled gloomily beneath the protecting branches of the horse-chestnut trees.

To everyone's relief, the sun struggled valiantly through a little after lunchtime. 'Thank goodness for that!' muttered Elaine to Danielle as she stepped from beneath the trees and held out her hand. 'Oh, good, it's stopped raining. Come on, let's go and sort those books out.'

They ran across the green, their sandals squelching in the wet grass, and pulled the plastic sheets from the bookstall. 'Well, at least the books are dry,' said Elaine. 'There's nothing quite like a soggy romance, is there? Oh, talking of romance, look who's here.' She nodded across the green.

Danielle turned just in time to see Nathan Stafford step from his car and stride across the green towards them. Just for a moment, taken unawares, she felt her heart seem to turn over at the sight of him in his smart pale-coloured suit.

Then she remembered that Elaine had said he was opening the fête. 'Hello, ladies.' He nodded at them both, but his eyes met Danielle's. 'I hope you've got the weather under control now. I don't think the vicar's included water sports in his schedule!' He paused and glanced round at the other stalls. 'I see our visitors from the common have joined us,' he observed.

Danielle nodded. 'Yes, but there's been friction already.' She went on to explain about the stalls. 'I just hope we get through the afternoon without a fight, that's all.'

'Well, I shall make a point of welcoming them to the annual fête in my opening speech,' said Nathan firmly.

Elaine giggled. 'I'd say that would make you very popular,' she said.

Nathan was as good as his word, and after he had declared the fête open Danielle was pleased to see that there seemed to be a crowd around the gypsies' stall.

The Lower Yarrow summer fête was always a

popular local event, and people came from miles around. Elaine and Danielle did a brisk trade on their bookstall, and they were so busy that by mid-afternoon Danielle had forgotten about the aggravations of earlier. She was reminded when Nathan suddenly appeared with plastic mugs of tea for herself and Elaine and a selection of iced cakes from the Women's Institute stall.

'I thought you might be in need of sustenance, together with a run-down on the latest gossip,' he said.

'Gossip?' Elaine's eyes rounded as if she couldn't believe that the usually reserved locum should be indulging in such a thing.

He grinned. 'Yes. Apparently the gypsies have taken more money on their stall than anyone else, and, as if that weren't enough, their children are winning all the races.'

'Oh, brilliant!' Elaine exploded with laughter, while Danielle gave a quiet smile as once again her eyes met Nathan's. This time, however, he didn't look away, and as she took the mug of tea from him his fingers touched hers. The feel of those cool, strong fingers seemed to release some chemistry, some hidden force between them, and for a moment Danielle felt helpless, incapable of movement or even of looking away.

Then the moment was gone as Elaine said, 'I bet old Ralph Flint's hopping mad. It looks as if most of that junk he bought is still on his stall.'

'It's not surprising,' said Nathan drily. 'Especially when someone found a "Made in Taiwan" sticker on one of his carved dophins. The stuff on the gypsies' stall is selling very well. I have to admit, some of it's beautifully crafted.'

'I really think the majority of the villagers don't mind them being here,' said Danielle, then, turning back to Nathan, she said, 'Have you heard any more about the petition?'

'Ah, I was saving that until last.' He smiled, and the look in his blue eyes started doing crazy things to her heart again. 'It seems that, when he didn't get anywhere with the council, Ralph Flint had a message faxed to the brigadier at his hotel.'

'He *what*?' Elaine's jaw dropped.

'Good heavens, he really does want to see the back of them, doesn't he?' said Danielle slowly. 'I wonder why he's so against them?' She looked quickly at Nathan. 'What did the brigadier say?'

'Well, that's the *pièce de résistance*, for, according to my source of information, the brigadier doesn't mind them being there, provided they aren't breaking the law.'

'Oh, that's wonderful!' Danielle clapped her hands.

Nathan grinned. 'I shouldn't get too excited—if they go on winning all the prizes today I should think they'd be run out of town.' He paused, then said, 'Have you got time to come and have a look round?'

Danielle hesitated and looked at Elaine, who nodded vigorously. 'Yes, off you go, I can manage here now.'

As she moved away with Nathan, Danielle was only too conscious of Elaine's speculative look and she knew she would have to face further interrogation later.

Slowly they strolled around the stalls, inspecting the goods that were left. The local butcher had set up a barbecue, and the aroma of sausages and fried onions wafted across the green, mingling with the more subtle scents from the gypsies' stall of dried herbs, lavender bags and pot-pourri.

Danielle bought some old-fashioned wooden clothes pegs from Barnaby, but as she paid him she became aware that someone else was watching her and Nathan. When she looked round she wasn't surprised to find Rollo's dark brooding gaze on her, and quickly she looked away.

Later they wandered to the far end of the green, where the children's sports were taking place, and it soon became evident to Danielle that Nathan hadn't been exaggerating when he'd said that the children from the common were winning all the prizes.

They watched the sack race and the three-legged race, then, as one of the smaller children won the egg and spoon race, Danielle realised that Nathan had grown very quiet.

Cautiously she glanced at him, and fleetingly, captured on his features as he watched the child who had won, was the same expression that she had seen when he had held the baby in his arms after the clinic at Pendleton.

She had wondered then what had triggered that expression, and she wondered now. Both times it had involved a child, and once again she found herself wondering if he had a child of his own; a child who had caused him anguish and heartbreak. Suddenly she longed to ask him, for at that moment he seemed to her to be very alone, very vulnerable, but she was unable to find the right words, and, even as she struggled, his attention was diverted and the opportunity was lost.

She turned her head and, seeing his frown, looked across the green to see what it was that had claimed his attention.

Two women were slowly approaching the gypsies' stall—one, tall, dressed in black with a scarlet shawl around her shoulders, was leaning heavily on an ebony walking stick, while the other, dressed in a loose floral dress, her black hair flowing, was walking as if every movement required a great effort.

'Shall we go and tell them that the brigadier said they can stay?' asked Danielle.

Nathan nodded. 'Why not? That poor girl looks as if she could do with cheering up.'

CHAPTER EIGHT

THE following morning Nathan picked Danielle up from her cottage at eleven o'clock. They had booked their ride for twelve-thirty, but Nathan had one or two outlying house calls and had asked Danielle if she minded going with him.

She had spent a restless night trying to come to terms with the strange effect Nathan was having on her, and by the morning she was ready to admit that if he'd asked she would probably have quite happily accompanied him to Timbuktu. The difficult part was understanding why she felt the way she did especially in view of the fact that when she had first met him she had as good as disliked him.

Now, however, it was a different matter, and that morning she had found herself getting ready with great care. She had bathed in water scented with apricot kernel and sweet almond oils, then dressed in jodhpurs and a white shirt. Her hair she had brushed until it shone, then caught it back from her face with two tiny slides. At the last moment she had picked up a quilted body-warmer because she knew that even in summer it could be cold on the top of the downs.

When she was ready she had critically surveyed herself in the hall mirror, trying to see herself through Nathan's eyes. She knew he was finding her increasingly attractive—the expression in his blue eyes had told her that—but she was uncertain what it was about her that he particularly liked.

She was still deliberating when the doorbell rang, and she jumped. Then, her heart beating madly, she opened the door, to find him on the step.

He smiled. 'Hello,' he said, and her breath caught in her throat. Briefly he allowed his eyes to travel over her, quite obviously liking what he saw. 'I'm afraid I don't have the proper gear for this,' he said apologetically.

'Don't worry,' she said, glancing at his denims and black sweat-shirt, 'you'll be fine. And Jennifer will lend you boots and a helmet.' Pausing just long enough to pick up her own helmet and riding crop from the hall table, she stepped outside and locked the cottage door.

Minutes later she was beside him in his car and they were heading out of the village. The unsettled weather of the previous day seemed to have passed, and the sun was shining brightly. There, was, however, a keen breeze, and soft fluffy clouds raced across the summer sky, while the daisies in the hedgerows looked taller than ever after their dousing.

'I only have two calls to make,' Nathan said after a while. 'John Griffiths is doing the on-call for the rest of the day.'

'Did he mind?' asked Danielle.

Nathan shook his head. 'No; in fact, he suggested it. Said it was time I had a day off.'

'Are you doing this locum during your leave?' she

asked curiously, suddenly wanting, needing to know everything about him, but at the same time frightened by what she might find out.

He hesitated for a moment, then said, 'Yes, I suppose you could say that. I've spent some time in Norfolk, so I've had a break.'

'How did you get to hear about this?'

'Judy Maitland is my cousin.'

She stared at him. 'I didn't know that. No one said anything.'

Nathan gave a slight shrug. 'Well, John certainly knows—I suppose it just didn't occur to him to mention it. He's a bit vague at times.'

'You could say that!' Danielle laughed.

'Judy and David came up to Norfolk for a weekend,' he went on after a few minutes. 'They mentioned this trip they'd planned to see David's folks in Australia and that they were having difficulty finding a locum. I said I didn't mind doing it, as I probably wouldn't be returning to Africa until the end of June.'

Danielle felt her heart jolt painfully at his words. So that was when he planned to return—the end of June—less than a month away.

'My mother wasn't too impressed with the arrangements,' he said abruptly.

Danielle turned her head to look at him and saw that the lines of tension were back on his face.

'I expect she was enjoying having you home for a while,' she said.

He nodded. 'Yes, that and the fact that I was supposedly under orders to take a complete break from medicine.' He had slowed the car as he was speaking, and, glancing up at a pair of cottages on a grassy bank above them, he said, 'Ah, here's the first call, Mr Mowbery—been having side-effects from his new medication for his Parkinson's. I won't be long.'

With that he was gone, leaving Danielle to wonder over what he had just said. Had he been ill? Was that what he had meant when he said he had been under orders to take a complete break? And if so, whose orders was he talking about? Could it be an employer, or. . .could it be a wife? She shrank from the thought. Elaine had said he wasn't married, but could she have been mistaken? He was, after all, extremely attractive.

While she sat and waited for him Danielle realised yet again how little she knew about this man who was beginning to take up so much of her thoughts, and before he returned to the car she had made up her mind that she really should use the time they would be spending together that day to try to find out some more about him.

When he got back into the car he said, 'I've put him back on to Sinemet-Plus—that suited him much better than the new drug. Now, what's next?' He glanced at his diary. 'Oh, yes, over to Stickworth Farm to see Mrs Morrell.'

'How is she?' asked Danielle, who knew the farmer's wife well from her visits to the surgery. She also knew that Daphne Morrell was terminally ill with cancer of the liver, which had followed the removal six years previously of a malignant melanoma from her thigh.

Nathan shook his head. 'It's only a matter of time. I want to make sure the pain is well controlled.'

'It's very sad for her family. They're so close,' said Danielle.

As they drew away from the Mowberys' cottage Danielle's attention was suddenly attracted by a splash of scarlet between the trees on the pathway ahead. At first she thought it was a cluster of poppies on the bank, but when they drew level she saw a young couple walking closely together, their arms around each other. The boy was scruffily dressed in tattered jeans and his long hair was tied back into a pony-tail, while the girl was dressed in a white suntop and shorts. The scarlet that had attracted Danielle's attention turned out to be a silk scarf that was tied around the girl's head, securing her long dark hair.

As they passed them Nathan looked into his driving mirror and frowned. 'Wasn't that Melanie Flint?'

'It was,' replied Danielle shortly.

'And wasn't the lad with her. . .?'

She nodded. 'From the common? He was.'

Nathan looked surprised for a moment, then he chuckled. 'I should think that would please her father,' he said.

'I can't imagine for one moment that her father knows,' said Danielle. 'But at least she doesn't seem to have suffered any ill effects from her fall, does she?'

'I wonder if that was the lad she was trying to impress when she came off her horse?' asked Nathan, shaking his head and still chuckling.

Fifteen minutes later, to the accompaniment of

squawking hens and barking dogs, they pulled into the yard of Stickworth Farm.

'Would you like to come in with me?' asked Nathan as he lifted his case out of the car.

'Yes, I would, if I may.' Danielle climbed out of the car just as Jack Morrell appeared at the entrance to the cowsheds.

'Morning, Doctor, Nurse Roberts.' He touched his cap, but Danielle noticed that his usual smile was missing.

They followed him into the farmhouse, where they were met by his daughter, Jill, a rosy-cheeked, sensible-looking girl in her early twenties. His son Robert was sitting at the kitchen table. He looked up as they entered, and Danielle thought it looked as if he'd been crying.

Jill took them through to a pleasant, sunny room at the back of the house which had been made into a bedroom for her mother.

Daphne Morrell was lying in bed, propped up by a mountain of pillows. She looked jaundiced, drawn and very ill, but she managed a smile for Danielle.

'How kind of you to come, Nurse Roberts,' she whispered, then, looking at Danielle's jodhpurs and boots, she added, 'and you on the way to the stables too.'

While Nathan drew up Mrs Morrell's injection of diamorphine and talked to Jill about the pain control, Danielle sat beside the bed and talked about the view of the garden from the window, the roses climbing the archway that led to the orchard and about Robert's A levels and his place at university.

Later, after they had left the farm and were climbing the steep lanes to Bagwich, Danielle remarked what a blow it would be to the Morrell family when Daphne died.

Nathan nodded. 'It will be, yes, but their closeness will see them through. I always feel it's families who are divided who suffer the most at times like this. The Morrells have a wealth of happy memories which will help to ease their grief, although they won't, of course, recognise that for quite some time.'

Danielle fell silent, wondering if what he had said about divided families bore any relation to her earlier theory that he might be divorced and separated from his children. Before she could even form her thoughts into any sort of question, however, he had changed the subject.

'I'm really looking forward to this ride,' he said as they turned into the track to the stables. 'Remind me which horse it is I'm to have.'

'Sultan.'

'And what's he like, Sultan?'

'Magnificent! He's black and lives up to his name in every way. In actual fact, you're highly honoured, Jennifer doesn't hire him out very often—she usually rides him herself. I think she was impressed when you said you rode to hounds—that's usually the measure of a good rider, in her book.'

'But not in yours, is that it?' His blue eyes were

teasing now as he brought the car to a halt in the stable yard, switched off the engine and turned to her.

'Not at all. I know it takes a competent rider to ride with a hunt, and I admire good riding—it's only the motive I don't agree with. Come on, let's go over to the tackroom and get you fixed up.'

They found Jennifer Herrington in the tackroom, and once she had kitted Nathan out with boots, a helmet and a crop she took them to the stalls, where they found the grooms saddling Sultan, and Poppy, a delightful chestnut mare.

While they waited Jennifer turned to Nathan. 'Was Melanie's X-ray all right?' she asked.

He nodded. 'Yes, it was fine, no signs of a fracture. In fact, we passed her a little while ago down in the village, so you needn't worry any further.'

'Well, that's a relief,' said Jennifer, pushing back her long fair hair, then bluntly added, 'Ralph Flint can be a nasty piece of work when he wants to be, and if Melanie had been hurt on my premises I don't doubt for one minute that he would have made life very unpleasant around here. Apparently, he absolutely dotes on the girl—I can't think why; as far as I'm concerned, she's a spoilt little brat. Ah, here are your mounts now.' She turned as the grooms led the two horses from their stalls.

Danielle glanced at Nathan to see his reaction as the huge stallion walked slowly across the cobbles. She was relieved to see the pleasure in his eyes as he eyed Sultan up and down, then she turned and stroked Poppy's nose as the mare whickered with recognition.

Within a few minutes they were mounted, girths were adjusted and Jennifer Herrington stood back, obviously satisfied that her beloved stallion was indeed in experienced hands. 'Have a good ride,' she called. 'It'll be marvellous up on the top today—I wish I were coming with you.'

They followed the chalk trail to the downs between acres of fresh green bracken, the horses' hoofs slipping from time to time on the loose, uneven surface, then, as they neared the top and the path opened out to rough heathland thick with heather and yellow gorse, the horses broke into a trot, anxious now to be away.

They held back until they were on the very crest of the downs, where the strong breeze tugged at their clothes, stung their cheeks and even pulled tendrils of Danielle's hair from beneath her helmet, and it was then that they broke into a canter.

Sitting well into her saddle, Danielle glanced across at Nathan as he rode alongside her, admiring the way he sat the stallion almost as if he and the horse were one. Then, as the horses strained forward, as if by mutual consent they gave them their heads and settled to a long exhilarating gallop across the miles of open downland.

As she felt the ripple of Poppy's powerful muscles beneath her and the taste of salt on her lips from the distant sea air Danielle felt her spirits soar.

They galloped for miles, only reining in when they reached a huge mound of rocks, and there in the shelter of the jagged stones they paused and looked down into the valley below.

'Look!' Danielle shouted, pointing with her crop. 'There's Pendleton over there, and there's Lower Yarrow to the left—you can just see the church.'

'Yes, and there's the circle of gypsy caravans on the common,' Nathan yelled back. He twisted in the saddle. 'I can't see Bagwich or the stables.' His voice was whipped away by the wind.

'What did you say?' she shouted.,

'I said I can't see Bagwich.'

'No, it's hidden behind the curve of the downs,' she replied, then, leaning forward in the saddle, she called, 'Do you see that copse down there? I'll race you!'

'OK—you're on!' He circled Sultan, but Danielle was away, galloping down across the short, springy heather towards the copse, which looked little more than an acid-green smudge at the foot of the downs.

It wasn't long, however, before she knew he wasn't far behind her, and, although she urged Poppy on, before they reached the copse the powerful black overtook them, as Danielle had guessed he would.

They thundered through the copse, lying along the necks of the horses to avoid low branches, then as Danielle approached a clearing in the trees she saw that Nathan had reined in, had turned and was waiting for her.

She had thought he might be triumphant at winning, but instead he praised her. 'You're an excellent horsewoman,' he said admiringly, and she flushed with pleasure. 'Jennifer Herrington taught you well.'

'Jennifer didn't teach me,' she said shortly, then without further explanation, she indicated an overgrown pathway on the far side of the clearing. 'Follow me,' she said. 'I want to show you something.'

They walked the horses in single file, almost forcing their way through the dense undergrowth for about half a mile to the far side of the copse, where once again the trees and undergrowth cleared, revealing the ruined shell of an old cottage.

It was almost hidden from view by weeds and a tangle of lupins and bramble that grew shoulder-high in what had once been the garden, while a mass of ivy and a wild creeping dog-rose tumbled over the crumbling stone of its outer walls.

They stopped, and Danielle leaned forward in her saddle. 'So it's still here,' she said. 'I thought perhaps the developers would have been in by now.'

She dismounted, and after only a moment's hesitation Nathan followed suit. They tethered the horses to a rotting gatepost, and immediately the two animals began to crop the lush grass that surrounded the cottage.

'What is this place?' Nathan stood back and stared up at the roof, part of which was gaping to the sky, its rafters exposed to the elements. 'Who lived here?'

Danielle shook her head. 'I don't know. It's been derelict for as long as I can remember. Let's have a look inside.'

The door had gone and the frame was rotten, the

wood splintered and green with age, and as they stepped inside there was a sudden flurry, and they jumped as two pigeons fluttered up from the rafters and flew out of the gaping hole above them. The flagstoned floor was splattered with bird droppings, while dandelions and purple thistles pushed up through the cracks and the dark corners were choked with wet leaves and mouse droppings.

'Someone's been here,' remarked Nathan, nodding towards the hearth, where the charred remains of a fire were visible.

'A tramp, most probably,' said Danielle. 'I shouldn't think anyone else would come here.'

'You've obviously been here before.'

She nodded. 'Yes, but many years ago now. I used to come here when I was a child.' She looked around as she spoke, as if she could conjure up scenes from the past in the stillness.

'With your gypsy friends,' he said quietly.

She nodded, and reached out her hand to touch the rotting window-frame, the glass long since gone. 'Yes, this was a magic place, a secret place that we thought only we knew about.'

'And was it your gypsy friends who taught you to ride like that?'

'Like what?'

'Like the wind and without fear.'

She allowed a smile to touch her lips. 'Yes, it was—they had their own horses in those days. Ezra was a horse dealer. I used to ride all the time, bareback more often than not.'

'I think I'm beginning to understand why these people mean so much to you,' he said staring down at her.

She nodded. 'That's true, I suppose they do. They were an important part of my childhood.'

'And Rollo—what was he?'

There was silence in the ruin, and even beyond there was only bird-song, the soft munching sound that the horses made as they chewed the grass, and the breeze whispering in the trees. She lowered her gaze. 'What do you mean?'

'He follows you everywhere with his eyes.'

Suddenly Danielle felt the now familiar sense of awareness sweep over her again; an overpowering awareness of the sheer masculinity of the man at her side.

'A long time ago Rollo thought he loved me,' she said, trying to keep her voice light.

'And you? How did you feel?'

'It was terribly romantic having a handsome gypsy boy in love with me—I was the envy of all the girls in the village school.'

'And what about now?' As he spoke Nathan stretched out his hand and with his fingertips he lightly touched the side of her jaw, just tilting her head enough so that he could look into her face.

'What do you mean?' she whispered, her whole body tensing at his touch.

'How do you feel about the handsome gypsy now that he's no longer a boy?'

'Nothing.' Her reply was firm. 'Rollo is married to Maria; he has a family.'

'No regrets?' he said softly. 'No regrets over lost fantasies?'

'Definitely not. Rollo was never meant for me, nor I for him—and, besides,' she lifted her eyes until they met his steady blue gaze, 'one surely creates new fantasies as the old ones die?'

'I'm glad you said that.' Slowly he leaned forward until his lips lightly touched hers.

His lips were cool and firm, and briefly she closed her eyes, frightened in this place of magic that he would become a figment of her imagination and disappear. But the next moment she felt his arms go round her, and the pressure from his lips increased, forcing her own lips apart. Hungrily she found herself responding as his kiss became more amd more demanding. She couldn't ever remember being kissed quite like this before, and when he finally drew away from her she only knew regret that it was over.

When she opened her eyes he cupped her face between his hands and was staring down at her.

'I almost accused you of witchcraft once,' he murmured. 'Now I know I wasn't far wrong, because you've totally bewitched me.'

Danielle felt a thrill shoot through her at his words, but he gave her no chance to reply, bringing his mouth down firmly on hers again.

CHAPTER NINE

THEY said very little on the ride back to Bagwich, but the enchantment of that precious moment in the cottage stayed with Danielle. She couldn't, however, help wondering what would happen when they returned to reality. How would Nathan behave? Would he act as if it hadn't happened? Maybe he would pretend it had just been a spontaneous reaction to the atmosphere, an action that wasn't to be repeated or pursued in any way.

As they rode into the stable yard Danielle threw him an anxious glance; his expression, however, was inscrutable, giving away nothing of his feelings. For herself, she knew that something momentous had happened and that for her, at least, life now would never be quite the same again.

For a moment in that magical environment she had been convinced that the kiss had meant as much to him as it had to her, and even afterwards, when he had held her close so that she had heard the steady beating of his heart. He had told her she had bewitched him, so she knew he had been as affected as she, but had that been an accusation? Had he wanted to be bewitched? Was it a condition he welcomed or one he would fight? Was he already bitterly regretting what had happened?

The comparative silence between them continued after they had returned the horses to their grooms and driven back through the steep lanes to Lower Yarrow. With a growing sense of desperation Danielle wondered what would happen when they reached Farthings. Would he merely bid her a cool goodbye and drive away?

Suddenly she doubted if she could bear that, and as Nathan brought the car to a halt in front of the cottage she scrabbled to unclip her seatbelt and get out of the car as quickly as possible.

'I'll see you in the surgery tomorrow,' she muttered as she opened the car door.

'Hey, just a moment. Why the hurry?'

She stopped and without turning to look at him said, 'I thought you wanted to get back. . .'

'And I thought you were going to ask me in.'

Slowly she turned her head and looked at him, and her heart turned over at the expression in his eyes. 'Oh, did you. . .?'

'I understood you were going to give me a massage after my ride.'

'Oh. . .I didn't say that. I mean, I didn't think. . .' Danielle trailed off, hot with embarrassment, then in a determined effort to pull herself together and appear professional she said, 'But yes, of course, if you'd like a massage. . .'

'I would, yes. Elaine told me how good you are and how much you helped her. It's been a long time since I've ridden a horse and I know I'll suffer during the next couple of days. I should be interested to see if you can help. Then afterwards I'd like you to come back to Foxworth with me for a meal.' As he spoke he climbed from the car, then as he locked the door he smiled at her across the roof. 'And don't worry, I've excelled myself and prepared a vegetarian meal.'

With that, the tension eased a little between them, although as she unlocked her front door and he followed her into the cottage Danielle was aware that her heart was beating very fast.

Between the living-room and the kitchen he had to duck his head so as not to hit himself on the low beam, and, as he looked around at her copper pans, her earthenware jars filled with dried flowers and the bunches of herbs hanging from the beams, a smile touched his lips and he nodded.

'Is there anything wrong?' She frowned.

'No, I was just thinking that this is exactly as I imagined it would be.' He glanced towards the staircase in the corner of the kitchen. 'It's a marvellous old place. How did you come by it?'

'It was my grandmother's,' she replied as she took fresh orange juice from the fridge and poured it into two glass tumblers. 'I was virtually brought up here. She knew how much I loved it, and when she died she left it to me.' She handed him one of the tumblers.

'I think I'm beginning to see why you're so happy living here in Lower Yarrow,' he said a little later as they sat at her kitchen table and sipped their orange juice. 'It's so peaceful that it's almost as if the rest of the world doesn't exist, as if we were in some sort of time warp.'

She laughed and set down her glass, and he glanced round the kitchen, taking in the old-fashioned Aga and, tucked away in one corner, the staircase that twisted up to the first floor.

'So where do you carry out your ministrations?' he asked.

She drained her glass and stood up. 'Come with me; I'll show you.'

He followed her up the stairs to the tiny guest room with its chintz curtains that she had converted for her massage and aromatherapy. Excusing herself for a moment, she went briefly into her own bedroom, where she changed out of her shirt and jodhpurs into a comfortable loose floral dress.

When she returned to the other room she found Nathan with his back to her, apparently intently studying her glass-fronted cabinet where she kept her stock of essential oils and her books on aromatherapy and herbal remedies. As she crossed to the handbasin to wash her hands she suddenly felt extremely nervous. This, she knew, was partly due to the fact that Nathan was a doctor and she had never practised her skills on a member of the medical profession before, but even stronger than that was the growing awareness between them; an awareness that had been there before today but which had exploded into sudden passion when he had kissed her.

'You have a large range of these oils,' he commented over his shoulder.

'Yes,' she agreed, wondering whether he would want a full massage or just his neck and shoulders. 'I have a fairly good stock now, but I still have a long way to go—some of the oils are incredibly expensive.'

'Do you mix them with anything?'

'Yes, I usually add several different essential oils, depending on the complaint I'm treating, to a vegetable base oil.'

'So what do you propose using on me so that I won't feel the after-effects of the ride?' There was a faintly amused expression in his blue eyes as he leaned back against the window-sill, folded his arms, stretched his long legs out before him and quizzically regarded her.

A shaft of sunlight had caught him, highlighting the golden flecks in his hair and accentuating his suntan. Danielle swallowed, trying hard to ignore the expression in his eyes, the sheer maleness of him and their inevitable close proximity in the confined space of the small bedroom. Desperately she attempted to adopt a businesslike, professional manner, not wanting him to even guess at the effect he was having on her.

'I shall use a combination of eucalyptus, peppermint and ginger oils in a base of sesame oil,' she said briskly as she unlocked the glass door of her cabinet and began selecting the phials she needed. What she didn't tell Nathan was that she also proposed to add some bergamot and geranium oils in the hopes of relieving some of the tension from which he seemed to have been suffering.

As she carried out her preparations, without looking at him, she said, 'Perhaps you'd like to take off your sweat-shirt and make yourself comfortable?'

She imagined he would simply sit on the one chair she had in the room, but when she turned she was surprised to find that he had removed his jeans as well as his sweat-shirt and was lying face down on the couch. His back was smooth, muscular and a deep golden brown, while his legs had a covering of dark bronzed hair.

Danielle took a deep breath; quite obviously he expected a full massage. Stepping towards the couch, she flexed her hands, poured a few drops of the prepared oil into her palm, then rubbed her hands together. For a moment her hands hovered above his naked back, then as her fingers touched his flesh he drew in his breath and tensed his muscles, then with a deep sigh released his breath.

Her nervousness disappeared almost as soon as she began the familiar rhythmic routine, and as her hands travelled over the contours of his body and the scents of the aromatic oils filled her senses she relaxed.

She quickly found and concentrated on the hard knot of muscles at the base of his neck that confirmed the presence of the suspected tension, and as she worked, her strong fingers moving in a series of firm circular movements on either side of his vertebrae, she physically felt him relax.

Applying more aromatic oil, she moved her attention to his back, then later, after only a moment's hesitation, to his hard, muscular thighs.

Throughout the massage Nathan was silent, his

head turned to one side, his eyes closed, the lashes dark against his cheek, and as she watched him Danielle felt her throat constrict in a sudden surge of tenderness. Who was this stranger who had walked into her life and taken command of her soul? Whoever he was, he had a lot to answer for, she thought as she ran her hands lightly up his back again, because he would no doubt simply walk out of her life as casually as he had come into it, back to whatever existence he had been living before, unaware of the turmoil he had caused and the havoc he would leave behind.

Almost as if he knew what she was thinking, Nathan, without opening his eyes, suddenly spoke. 'Elaine was quite right about your expertise,' he said quietly. 'I haven't felt so relaxed in a very long time.'

Danielle hesitated fractionally, then, taking advantage of the situation and rapidly coming to a decision, said, 'Have you been ill recently?'

He opened his eyes then. 'Not exactly. Why do you ask?'

'You had a tremendous amount of tension in your neck and shoulders.'

He didn't reply, and as she almost reluctantly brought the massage to an end she added, 'And you mentioned before that you'd been told to take a break. I just wondered if you'd been ill.'

Nathan took a deep breath. 'I suppose I've been suffering from what's fashionably known as burn-out.'

'And what's caused that?' She held her breath as she waited for his reply, dreading what she might be about to hear about his private life.

He didn't answer immediately, however, instead turning, and sitting on the edge of the couch looking up at her.

She tried not to look at the dark triangle of hair on his chest that tapered off to a point disappearing beneath his shorts.

'Do you have any theories about what might have caused it?' he asked softly. 'After all, at the moment I'm your patient.' There was briefly a note of amusement in his tone, but it was gone almost immediately and he was serious again.

'How can I even hazard a guess? I hardly know anything about you. . .' She hesitated. 'I did wonder. . .' She trailed off, embarrassed, but Nathan reached out and caught her hand. At the touch of his fingers she stiffened.

'Yes?' he prompted. 'What did you wonder?'

Again she hesitated, unsure how to put her suspicions into words, but she looked down into the blueness of his gaze and suddenly, because of the intimacy they had shared, it was easy.

'I wondered if your tension had been caused by a woman,' she said simply, then added, 'and then on other occasions I found myself wondering if children were involved.'

He stared at her, still holding her hand. 'Why did you think that?'

'I'm. . .I'm not sure. It was something to do with the way you are with children, the way you look at them, the way you hold them. . .it was almost as if. . .' her voice faltered, then she carried on '. . .as if you perhaps have children of your own from whom you've been parted.'

He was silent as she finished speaking, then he dropped her hand, stood up and walked towards the window. She watched him in dismay, thinking she had gone too far, said too much, that the pent-up anger was back and that the last hour had been a waste of time.

'Nathan. . .? I'm sorry,' she began, stepping towards him and reaching out her hand to touch his bare shoulder.

At her touch, however, he turned towards her, and the expression in his eyes made her stop.

'It's all right, Danielle,' he said huskily. 'I'll tell you what it's all about.' He turned his face again towards the window, but a far-away look had come into his eyes and she suspected that the scene below in her garden was not the one he was seeing in his mind.

'You were right in a way when you said you thought my problems might be due to a woman and children.' A tight little smile touched his lips, but Danielle felt her heart sink at his words. 'But it isn't in the way you think.'

She frowned. 'What do you mean?'

'The woman is not a flesh-and-blood woman.'

'I don't understand.'

His features tightened. 'The woman is Africa and the children aren't mine personally—they're the millions who are starving of hunger—but I care as much about them as if they were my own. Caring for them, working with them, I know, has become an obsession, and I've driven myself to the absolute limits. My anger comes from knowing how little I can achieve, and I have to consciously stop myself from comparing how much the children here have. Don't get me wrong,' he glanced quickly at her, 'I don't begrudge any child anything, but when I think of the constant struggle we have just to keep them alive. . .when every grain of rice is counted. . .when whole families walk hundreds of miles through the desert in search of food, only to find there is none. . .' The far-away look was back in his blue eyes and she knew he was seeing once again that vast desert with its endless columns of people drifting aimlessly in search of food. A scene she herself had agonised over when she had watched television documentaries but which she had never before heard about at first hand.

'The story's still grim even for those we do manage to save,' he continued, sensing her deep interest, 'for after malnutrition there's always dysentery, cholera, gastroenteritis. . .the list is endless, and at times it all seems hopeless, for just when famine relief arrives for one area it seems that within months another area is afflicted.'

'But you are totally dedicated in your fight?' she asked softly.

He turned and looked at her, refocusing his vision as if returning from some far-off place. 'Yes,' he sighed, 'yes, I suppose I am.'

She gave a faint smile. 'And there was me, thinking

that you wouldn't understand my standing up for the gypsies.'

'Oh, I understand, only too well. I've been fighting one cause or another ever since I was a child, as my mother would no doubt tell you if she had the chance.'

'I gather your mother wasn't too happy at your coming here?'

Nathan shook his head, then grinned. 'No, she wasn't. My medical officer had sent me home with strict instructions to rest. He said I was suffering from exhaustion. Unfortunately my mother found out and started fussing around, to such an extent that when Judy and David said they were looking for a locum I jumped at the chance just to escape. My mother was horrified, but the ironic part is that normally she would have been delighted.'

'Why is that?' Danielle looked up curiously, marvelling at how much he had opened up and how much he was telling her about himself.

'She's always living in hopes that I'll get married and settle down to the quiet, respectable life of a village GP, just like David.'

'And all the time the only woman in your life is Africa,' said Danielle softly.

'I didn't say she was the only woman.' She raised her eyebrows enquiringly, and he gave a teasing smile. 'There have been others.'

'I can imagine. . .'

'But none could stand the pace. . .' He smiled, then sighed. 'Seriously, there aren't many women who would want my lifestyle. . .a desert camp in a bush station, a hundred and one degrees in the shade and a social life equal to none.' He gave a short laugh.

'And how soon is it before you return to all that?'

'Very soon,' he replied, and she couldn't help but notice the spark that flared in his blue eyes.

'You sound as if you can't wait to get back.' Danielle tried to disguise the note of reproach in her voice, but it was there, and as Nathan glanced quickly at her she knew he had detected it.

'You're right, I couldn't wait to get back—that was, until I came to a sleepy little English village where there seems to be magic in the air. He leaned towards her slightly as he spoke and, lifting his hands, gently cupped her face and tilted it to his. 'Or maybe it's witchcraft. I don't know, but, whatever it is, suddenly I'm not in quite as much of a hurry to return to the heat and sand as I was.'

As Danielle stared up at him she held her breath, then the expression in his eyes grew more intense, his lips parted and she sighed as for the second time that day his mouth covered hers. While one hand held her jaw, the fingers caressing the side of her face, the other became entangled in her hair as the pressure from his lips intensified.

Vaguely she was aware that he had eased her backwards against the window-sill, and as his hard, taut body strained against hers she gripped the edge of the sill behind her, then his arms went round her, crushing her against him, and with a sigh she entwined her own arms around his neck, burying her fingers in his thick hair.

The kiss lasted a long time, evoking desires in Danielle that she never dreamt existed, and when at last they drew reluctantly apart Nathan too seemed shattered by the depths of emotion they had reached.

In an obvious attempt to lighten the tension between them he stepped back and looked down into her face. 'Do you treat all your patients like this?' he asked, but the huskiness in his tone confirmed the fact that he too was shaken by what had happened between them.

'It certainly isn't very professional, is it?' she said ruefully. 'I could probably get struck off for this, Dr Stafford.'

'Oh, I don't know, it probably doesn't count because I'm a doctor and I won't say anything, provided you promise you won't extend the same service to any of your other patients. Besides, it's my turn now. You're coming back to Foxworth for that meal I promised.'

When they left Farthings Danielle felt as if her senses were singing. Somewhere some hidden sixth sense was urging caution, telling her not to get involved with this man, for, in spite of the fact that he had told her he wasn't married, she knew deep in her heart that it would be madness to lose her heart to him. By his own admission, his heart was in his work, in Africa, a continent to which very soon he would be returning, but that particular night she knew she would throw caution to the winds.

She had never been happier, for Nathan Stafford had awakened desires that yearned for fulfilment, had given her a hint of undreamed-of pleasure, of a passion that had lain dormant until now, almost as if it had been waiting only for him.

In such a short space of time so much had been explained regarding his attitudes, and Danielle felt she now knew him and understood him so much better.

It was a mellow early evening, and as Danielle shut her cottage gate to join Nathan in his car she noticed old Hilton Miles crossing the village green, his sack over his shoulder and his Jack Russell terrier at his heels. He raised one hand in greeting, then disappeared down the dark overgrown pathway that led to the woods. She took her seat beside Nathan and he nodded towards the path.

'Does a spot of poaching, does he?'

Danielle laughed. 'Yes, and he has done for as long as anyone can remember. No one seems to take any notice.'

'Well, he certainly seemed to know who owns the land round here.'

They drew away and took the longer route to the common up the lane past Dr Griffiths' surgery. Nathan parked the car at the side of Foxworth, and as they walked round to the front of the house that overlooked the common he slipped his arm around her shoulders.

All seemed quiet on the common. Even the children who were usually at play on the grass were missing, and the doors to the caravans were closed, but as they turned into the short drive that led up to the old stone house Danielle had the feeling that they were being watched.

She turned briefly and scanned the silent caravans, the patches of sunlight on the grass and the lengthening shadows from the woods beyond, but nothing moved. The only sound was the cooing of wood-pigeons, and there was not a soul to be seen.

They walked a short way up the drive, and Nathan moved his hand from her shoulder to the nape of her neck, gently caressing and working his fingers.

'It feels as if you could be good at massage,' she said softly.

They laughed, and the sound hung in the silent air as Nathan took the key from his pocket and stepped forward to open the front door.

While she waited Danielle turned again and glanced back at the common, and this time she saw a movement in the dark shadows from a clump of sycamores and she knew her suspicion had been correct. Her intuition told her that it was Rollo who was there; that he had stood silently in the shadows and had watched her come back with Nathan. That he was still there, watching, as Nathan turned and took her hand, leading her into the empty house.

CHAPTER TEN

Foxworth was a quietly elegant yet comfortable family home with much evidence of David and Judy Maitland's three children and their variety of animals. The household seemed to revolve around the vast kitchen, with its pine dresser loaded with blue delft china and the large refectory table. One wall was almost entirely given over to children's paintings and an immense notice board packed with information ranging from school meetings to dental appointments, from the local plumber's phone number to birthday reminders. A Victorian-style conservatory led off the kitchen, furnished with padded cane chairs and a white wrought-iron table. The red marbled floor tiles were dotted with dozens of tubs of well tended plants, while hanging baskets suspended from the ceiling trailed their contents in colourful cascades.

'Judy does love her plants,' observed Danielle admiringly from the conservatory doorway.

'Yes,' agreed Nathan from the kitchen, then added, 'Trouble is, I'm in charge of them while she's away— I'm terrified they're all going to die on me.'

'They look healthy enough.'

'That's true,' he agreed, then added, 'and it isn't for much longer, so I shouldn't get involved with anything technical like re-potting.'

Danielle joined in his laughter, but his comment had only served to remind her once again how little time they had before he went away. With a little stab of misery she turned away from the conservatory and watched him as he began taking food from the fridge.

He had obviously taken pains over the food he had chosen for their meal, as to her surprise he set out stuffed peppers, watercress and orange salad, fresh crusty bread and butter, strawberries and cream and a bottle of sparkling white wine.

And it was then, in that very moment as she watched him and recognised the trouble he had taken to please her, that Danielle knew she loved him.

He poured a glass of wine, handed it to her and smiled, his eyes meeting hers over the rim of his glass, and she reached a decision; for that evening at least she would ignore the voice inside that cautioned her against involvement with this man, and she wouldn't later regret whatever happened between them.

Whether or not he read her decision in her eyes she didn't know, but his gaze held hers for a long time, then deliberately he set down his glass and, walking round the pine table, he once again gathered her into his arms, and she willingly gave herself up to another of his kisses.

This time his actions became more demanding, his lips more possessive and his hands more adventurous as they roamed over her body, at first lightly caressing her hips, her thighs, drawing her closer to him so that she felt the answering response from his own body, then moving, cupping her breasts and finding the nipples taut with desire beneath the thin cotton fabric of her dress. Until at last, when she was heady with unfulfilled passion, Nathan pulled away with a groan.

'You're doing it again,' he muttered in a conscious effort to control himself. 'You're bewitching me.'

She threw back her head, shaking the hair from her eyes, revealing the whiteness of her throat, then she heard him catch his breath before he reached out for her again and pulled her roughly into his arms once more.

It was some time later, when her body was still aching with desire for him, and her nerves were taut with anticipation of what was to come, that they took their food into the conservatory, and threw open the doors to the soft evening air, and for the next hour or so they ate the meal Nathan had prepared and drank the sparkling wine.

And all the while Danielle was hardly able to take her eyes from Nathan, could hardly believe what was happening between them, but at the same time refusing to consider the future.

Then later, as the sun was sinking behind the scots pines on the fringe of the common and the air was fragrant with the scents from the garden, Nathan stood up and reached out his hand to her. Unhesitatingly she put her hand in his, and as she stood up he pulled her to him, holding her against him for a moment of stillness. Then, putting his hand beneath her chin, he tilted her face towards his, searching her features then staring down into her eyes as if he wanted to read the workings of her very soul.

'Are you sure?' he murmured at last. 'Are you sure this is what you want?'

'I've never been surer in my life,' she whispered, then, anticipating his protest as he opened his mouth to speak, she reached up and put her fingers across his lips. 'No, don't say it. . .I know you can't promise me anything. I know you have to go back, but I accept that. We both want this—let's just share this moment and enjoy the time we have together.'

In spite of her words of reassurance, he still seemed to hesitate, then as she gently traced her fingers down his face she softly said, 'But are you sure that this is what you want?'

'I can't ever remember wanting anything more.' His voice was low, husky, and she thrilled at its note of urgency. 'I've never felt quite like this before about anyone, Danielle.' He said it wonderingly, as if he couldn't believe what was happening to him.

She laughed. 'Well, you did accuse me of witchcraft!' Sliding her hands round his neck, she pulled his face down and pressed her lips against his.

It was the sound of frantic knocking at the front door that brought them abruptly back to reality.

'What the hell's going on. . .?' muttered Nathan, pulling reluctantly away from Danielle, then, leaving her to re-button her dress, he turned and disappeared into the hall just as the knocking began again.

There was something about the urgency of the sound that made Danielle follow Nathan, and as he pulled open the front door she stared in amazement as she saw Sophia on the step.

The gypsy woman was clearly out of breath and she rested one clenched fist on the door-frame as if for support.

All she said was, 'It's Maria,' but it was all that was needed.

Nathan gave a muttered exclamation before telling her to wait while he got his case from the study. As he briefly disappeared Sophia looked up and saw Danielle.

'Is it the baby, Sophia?' asked Danielle urgently, noticing the fear that flickered in the older woman's black eyes.

She nodded and, still gasping for breath, she said, 'It's going wrong—she's bleeding, and I can't stop it.'

As Nathan joined them Danielle said, 'I'll come with you; I may be able to help.'

As they left Foxworth Nathan ran on ahead, leaving Danielle to help Sophia, who hobbled painfully across the uneven grassy surface of the common.

'She wasn't like this with the other two,' muttered Sophia as she struggled to keep up with Danielle.

'Is Rollo with her?'

The gypsy woman shook her head and her mouth tightened. 'I don't know where he is,' she said grimly, her fingers clutching at her red shawl.

When they reached Sophia's caravan they found several of the other women in a huddle round the steps, gossiping excitedly. When they caught sight of Sophia they fell silent and parted to allow her and Danielle access to the caravan.

As they stepped inside, the sight that met their eyes

was even worse than Danielle had feared. In the living area of the caravan Maria's two young children sat huddled together on a sofa, their eyes huge with terror as they listened to the sounds of moaning coming from the sleeping quarters beyond.

When Danielle investigated further she found Maria lying on the couch-type bed, surrounded by blood-soaked towels. She was deathly pale, with dark rings under her eyes. As Danielle stood in the doorway Nathan straightened up from examining Maria.

'I can still hear the foetal heart,' he said, then, opening his case, he took out his radio and, passing a bag of saline to Danielle, indicated for her to start setting up an intravenous drip.

'Can you help her?' gasped Sophia, who had followed Danielle into the caravan.

'I want her in hospital immediately,' said Nathan.

'No. . .Rollo wouldn't let her go. . .' began Sophia, but Nathan ignored her and began radioing for an ambulance.

As he waited for a reply he glanced up at Danielle and nodded towards the other room. 'Can you organise those children before the ambulance arrives?'

She nodded, and when Nathan had finished giving his message to ambulance control he took over the drip from her, and she went outside, where she asked the women around the steps if they would take the two young children and look after them.

There were nods and murmurs among the women, then two of them followed her back into the caravan and lifted Maria's two boys from the couch and carried them away, presumably to their own caravans.

When Danielle returned to the bedroom she found Nathan questioning Sophia as to what she had given Maria in the way of medication.

'I gave wild arrach to ease her womb, then later fennel for the pain, and when the bleeding started I was going to give snakewort, because she hasn't reached her time yet.' She looked at Nathan. 'What do you think?'

'It's a little late for snakewort, Sophia,' he said briskly, but his tone was not unkind. 'What we have here is an antepartum haemorrhage, and what Maria needs is a Caesarian section and a transfusion.'

Sophia shook her head and, lowering her voice so that the moaning girl on the bed wouldn't overhear, she said, 'Rollo won't want that.'

'You're saying he'd rather lose his child and possibly his wife?'

Sophia began twisting her wrinkled hands together in agitation, and Danielle, feeling suddenly sorry for her, took her hands in hers. 'Listen, Sophia, you've done your best for Maria, Rollo will know that, but there are times when maybe your medicine just isn't enough—times when you need help.'

Still the woman shook her head, then Danielle said, 'You don't want to lose Maria, just as you lost Ezra, do you?'

At the mention of her elder son's name Sophia's brown features crumpled. 'Ezra should have gone to hospital,' she muttered. 'Everyone thought I could save him, but I didn't know how.'

Maria suddenly cried out, and Sophia looked wildly around. 'Oh, I wish Rollo were here!' she cried.

'Where is he?' asked Nathan, turning from the bed.

'I don't know.' Sophia shook her head. 'He was here earlier, then he just disappeared, went off on his own without telling anyone where he was going. Soon after that Maria's pains started. . .'

For a fraction of a second Nathan's eyes met Danielle's across the bed, and she wondered briefly whether he too had been aware of the watcher in the shadows when he had taken her into Foxworth with the intention of making love to her. Had it been Rollo? Had he seen them? Had he with his uncanny perceptiveness known what was happening? Had it affected him to see her with Nathan, and if so had he taken himself off somewhere to cool his anger at the very moment when his wife went into labour and needed him beside her?

Even as the questions chased themselves through her brain, Danielle heard the sound of a klaxon as the ambulance raced down the lane towards the common.

Under Nathan's direction the ambulance men carried Maria out of the caravan on a stretcher into the waiting ambulance. They were watched by a silent throng, who stood in little groups in the gathering dusk among their caravans.

'Shall I come with you?' Danielle asked Nathan as he prepared to climb into the back of the ambulance.

He nodded. 'Yes, please. I think Maria would like to have you there.' He paused and looked back to where Sophia stood at the top of her caravan steps, watching them. 'Would you like to come, Sophia?'

The gypsy woman shook her head, as Danielle had suspected she would. 'No, Dani, go. It's best if I be here when Rollo comes back.'

Nathan nodded, then followed Danielle into the ambulance, and moments later they were on the way to the hospital.

While Nathan kept a close watch on the bleeding, Danielle administered Entinox to Maria to help ease the pain, at the same time sitting by her side and holding her hand while she held the mask in place.

Once the gypsy girl opened her eyes and seemed aware of Danielle.

'It's all right, Maria,' Danielle whispered, pushing back the damp black hair from her forehead, 'everything's going to be just fine.'

The girl sighed and closed her eyes again, and Danielle found herself silently cursing Rollo for not being there.

They reached the hospital within twenty minutes, thanks to the skill of the driver, and Maria was taken straight to the obstetrics wing, where she was immediately prepared for Theatre.

Danielle waited in Sister's office, and was later joined by Nathan, who explained what was happening.

'She's to have a Caesarian section,' he said. 'I'm afraid she's in rather a bad way.'

'I think I'd like to stay,' said Danielle.

'I thought you'd say that. I'll see if I can organise some coffee for us.'

'Oh, you don't have to stay. . .' she began, then stopped when she saw his expression.

'You don't think I'm going to clear off and leave you here, do you? Besides, I should say that poor girl needs all the support she can get at the moment. Her family don't seem to exactly be falling over each other to rush to her side.'

'You mustn't blame them,' she said quickly. 'They don't understand all this.' She waved her hand, indicating the hospital.

He smiled. 'Always ready to rush to their defence, aren't you?'

Danielle sighed as he disappeared out of the office in search of some coffee. Did he think her foolish, standing up for these people? But then, hadn't he said that he was always ready to fight a cause? Wasn't that in effect what he was doing in Africa? A sudden wave of misery swept over her as she thought of his work and of how it seemed to be the driving force in his life, and that he would soon be returning to that and going out of her life, possibly forever.

Earlier she had been prepared to dismiss these worries and live for the present, but deep down she knew that if she allowed herself to become any closer to Nathan she was putting herself in danger of never recovering.

The wait seemed endless, then eventually the obstetrician came to the office to find them.

Danielle looked up anxiously but could read nothing from his expression. He had obviously met Nathan on a previous occasion, for he seemed to know that he was Dr Maitland's locum. He also seemed curious about Maria Lees.

'Had she had any antenatal care?' he asked Nathan as he perched on the edge of Sister's desk and flicked through some notes.

Nathan shook his head. 'Not authentic care,' he said.

'What do you mean?' The older man frowned and peered at Nathan over his bifocals.

Nathan glanced at Danielle. 'Perhaps Nurse Roberts will explain—she knows the Lees family better than I do.'

'Maria's part of a travelling family, a Romany, in fact,' said Danielle. 'The only care she'll have had will have been their own herbal remedies.'

The obstetrician nodded thoughtfully. 'I wondered if it was something like that.'

'Is she all right?' Danielle found herself holding her breath.

'What?' Again he peered absent-mindedly over his glasses.

'Maria Lees—is she all right?' repeated Danielle.

'Oh, yes, she'll be OK. . .now,' he paused and glanced through his notes again, 'but I must admit it was touch and go there for a while.'

'And the baby?'

'Yes, a fine, healthy girl. . .surprising, really, in the circumstances.'

'Can I see her for a moment?' asked Danielle with a sigh of relief. She had been dreading the thought of having to give Rollo any bad news.

'I should think Sister could arrange that.'

Leaving Nathan to talk to the obstetrician, Danielle followed Sister into a small side-room off the main maternity ward.

'Mrs Lees has just come round,' explained Sister, 'so we've brought her baby to be with her for a few moments. The baby will, of course, be returned to the special baby-care unit afterwards.'

A shielded single light was burning above the bed where Maria, her black hair spread around her, appeared to be sleeping peacefully. Danielle approached the bed and peeped into the crib alongside, where all that was visible was a tuft of black hair beneath a white shawl, then as she stared down at the girl on the bed Maria opened her eyes.

'Dani. . .?' Her voice was soft and sleepy, and Danielle had to bend over her to hear what she said next. 'Do. . .do you know where Rollo is?'

Danielle bit her lip, then shook her head. 'No, dear, I don't at the moment, but I'm sure he'll be in to see you as soon as he hears about his new daughter.'

Maria sighed, then her eyes closed again. Danielle stood watching her for a few moments, then as she turned she realised that Nathan was standing behind her, looking down into the crib.

'They'll be all right now,' he said softly.

'Thanks to you,' she whispered. 'If it hadn't been

for your swift actions I doubt whether either of them would have made it.'

He shrugged. 'I wish my actions could always produce such satisfactory results.' He turned, and as Danielle followed him from the room, pulling the door to behind her, she knew that he was referring to the many babies in Africa he had been powerless to help.

It was very late when they left the hospital, and Nathan phoned for a taxi to take them back to Lower Yarrow. As she sat beside him in the rear seat Danielle suddenly felt overwhelmingly tired. It had been a strange day in many ways, and she knew she wouldn't be sorry to simply shut her eyes and give in to sleep.

As they approached the village, however, Nathan suddenly turned to her. 'Do you want to go straight to the cottage?'

'Perhaps I should,' she began, wondering if he had meant to return to Foxworth and continue where they had left off when Sophia had interrupted them, then her hand flew to her mouth. 'Oh, I can't—I've just remembered we were in such a hurry that I left my handbag at Foxworth. The keys to the cottage are in it.'

'Very well,' said Nathan calmly, leaning forward to speak to the driver, 'we'll go to Foxworth.'

There was something in his tone that made her heart leap, and moments later he was helping her out of the taxi.

While she waited for him to pay the driver she stood in the lane and looked towards the common.

Everything was in darkness, and she wondered if Rollo had returned. Suddenly she felt angry with him. If he had come back, why hadn't he contacted the hospital? On the other hand, maybe he was still out. She was tempted to go over to the caravans and tell them the good news, but it was almost two o'clock, and she and Nathan had already agreed that they would wait until morning before rousing anyone.

The taxi drove off down the lane, and as the sound of its engine receded and the gleam from its headlights grew fainter all was silent.

Nathan turned and took her hand; an owl hooted in the woods beyond the common and some small creature scurried into the hedge beside them. They walked up the short drive, Danielle resting her head on Nathan's shoulder, then he opened the front door and she followed him inside. He flicked on the light switch, and for one moment, a single moment of disbelief, they stared around them.

Nathan recovered first. 'My God!' he said. 'What the devil's been happening here?'

CHAPTER ELEVEN

IN GROWING horror they investigated the Maitlands' lovely old home. In the bedrooms and on the ground floor furniture had been upturned, the contents of cupboards and drawers pulled out and strewn around. In the kitchen, jars and canisters of food had been emptied into a sticky mass on the table, and in David's study hundreds of books had been pulled from their shelves and thrown into a heap in the centre of the floor. But the most heartbreaking sight was in the conservatory, where Judy's precious plants had been upturned or in some cases snapped off and trampled underfoot. The conservatory door was wide open to the darkness of the garden beyond.

'That's where they got in,' said Nathan grimly. 'I must have left it open, we went in such a hurry.'

'Do you think they've taken much?' asked Danielle, staring around her, shocked by the senseless vandalism.

'It's going to be the devil of a job finding out,' replied Nathan, shaking his head as he surveyed the damage, then suddenly his eyes narrowed and he crossed the conservatory and retrieved a handbag from under an asparagus fern that had been knocked to the ground. 'This is yours, isn't it?' He turned to Danielle as he spoke and held out the bag.

'Yes, it is.' She took it from him, opened it and peered inside.

'Is there anything missing?'

'I don't think so. . .wait a minute.' She tipped out the contents on to the wrought-iron table, which seemed to be the only piece of furniture still in its orignal position, then she frowned. 'That's odd,' she said slowly as she went carefully through her belongings.

'What is?' Nathan turned sharply. 'Are your keys there?'

She nodded. 'They are, and so is my purse with fifteen pounds inside, and this gold bracelet, which I took off when we went riding.' She glanced up. 'It's almost as if they were after something in particular and weren't interested in anything else.'

'Either that or they were hell-bent on causing as much damage as they could,' said Nathan grimly. 'And if that was the case it looks as if they've succeeded.'

'I wonder who's responsible? Do you think it could have been someone who saw us go out. . .?' began Danielle, then as it dawned on her what she was saying she threw Nathan a half-fearful glance. She saw immediately that the same thought had occurred to him.

He drew in his breath sharply. 'Well, if this is the work of our travelling friends then by God they're not going to get away with it! I've given them the benefit of the doubt until now, but this really is the limit!' As he spoke he turned and strode back into the sitting-room, where he found the telephone miraculously still connected and lifted the receiver.

'Nathan. . .' Danielle followed him. 'Nathan, I can't believe they did this. Why, we were helping them, helping Maria, and they all must have known that. . .' She trailed off, biting her lip.

'Yes, all except one,' said Nathan through clenched teeth. 'And where was he? Sulking in some jealous rage because he saw us together? I'm sorry, Danielle, I know they're your friends, but Judy and David are mine. This is a matter for the police now.' He dialled a number, and Danielle looked on in misery. She had never seen Nathan so angry, and she knew he had just cause.

He spoke to the police, then replaced the receiver. 'They'll be right round. They said not to touch anything.'

They didn't have long to wait before the ghostly blue light of the approaching police car eerily lit the lane outside and two officers arrived.

After they had questioned Nathan and examined the damage, one of the officers asked if either Nathan or Danielle suspected anyone, anyone who might be harbouring a grudge either against them or the Maitlands.

Danielle remained silent. Nathan shot her an uncomfortable glance, his anger partly abated, but before he had the chance to say anything the second officer said, 'Have you had any trouble with your neighbours?' He jerked his head in the direction of the common, leaving them in no doubt as to whom he meant.

Nathan hesitated for only a few more seconds, then he said, 'Well, now you ask, yes, there have been a few incidents since they arrived.'

'Right, Doctor, I think we'll have a few words with our hippy friends.'

'Now or in the morning?' asked Danielle anxiously.

'I think it'd better be now, love. If we leave it until daylight we could very well find that our friends have done a moonlight flit.' The officer turned to Nathan. 'Do your best to see what's missing, Doctor, but if you can't it'll have to wait until the owners of the property return.'

'Can we clear up now?' asked Danielle.

'Yes.' The officer looked round. 'I don't envy you—a right mess they've made!'

After the police had gone they straightened up the furniture, then Nathan sighed and pulled his hand wearily across his face. 'I don't think we should do any more tonight—we must get some rest. We both have surgeries in the morning.'

Danielle nodded. By this time she was so tired that she was almost beyond thinking. 'I'll come and help you to get straight after work tomorrow,' she said.

'Come on, I'll walk you back to the cottage.'

The first pearly streaks of dawn were lighting the sky as they left the house, and the tail-lights of the police car were visible as it travelled slowly up the lane and there were several lights on in the caravans.

The door of Sophia's caravan stood open, and as

they approached she appeared in a dressing-gown, her hair hanging over her shoulder in a long single plait.

She frowned and screwed up her eyes, then when she realised it was them an anxious expression crossed her dark features. 'Maria. . .?' she began.

'It's all right, Sophia,' said Danielle quickly. 'Maria's fine—she's had a lovely daughter.'

'So what was wrong? The bleeding?'

Nathan answered. 'It was what we call a placenta praevia, which means that the afterbirth was coming away first.'

'Ah.' The gypsy woman nodded as if she accepted that what had happened had been beyond her capabilities, then thoughtfully she said, 'So Rollo has the daughter he always wanted. . .'

'Where is your son, Sophia?' asked Nathan, and this time the gentleness was missing from his tone.

'I don't know.' Sophia shrugged. 'The police asked if there's any man in my family. I tell them, Rollo, he comes and goes. You know that.' She looked keenly at Danielle. 'He has always been the same. Sometimes he goes off for days at a time. Isn't that right?'

Danielle nodded. 'Yes, Sophia, that's quite right,' she agreed. But what she didn't add was that when Rollo used to take himself off it was usually after some disagreement or when he couldn't have things his own way.

'You do know what's happened tonight at Foxworth?' said Nathan.

Sophia nodded, 'Yes, I know, and I'm sorry,

Doctor. You're a good man, and it shouldn't have happened to you.' She gave a deep sigh and tightened her dressing-gown around her. 'We shall be blamed, as always.' With that she turned and went back into her caravan, pulling the door shut behind her.

Danielle only managed to get two hours' sleep before she had to get up for work. When she awoke she felt heavy-headed and depressed, and as she prepared for work she realised that during the excitement of the night somehow the magic that had been between herself and Nathan had dissolved. He had only given her a perfunctory kiss on the forehead when he had left her at the gate, and she had felt a wave of misery as she had watched him walk away. No doubt he too had been exhausted, but she had the feeling that what had happened had somehow put a barrier between them.

The sky that morning was heavy and overcast, the air humid, doing nothing to improve Danielle's lethargy, and when she reached the surgery she found Elaine agog with the half-rumours she had heard that morning.

'So what really happened?' she demanded as Danielle gratefully accepted the offered cup of coffee. 'Winnie Hobart in the shop said she'd heard you were involved.'

'Only in that I went in the ambulance with Maria Lees and stayed at the hospital until her baby was delivered.'

'And what about Dr Stafford?' Elaine obviously wanted all the details.

'Yes, he was there too.'

'And then there was something about a break-in.'

'That's right. When we got back from the hospital we found that Foxworth had been broken in to.'

'Did they take much?' Elaine's eyes were growing rounder by the minute.

'Nathan wasn't sure—it's very hard to tell when it's someone else's property.'

'Yes, I suppose it is,' agreed Elaine, then added, 'Of course, everyone's saying it's the gypsies.'

Danielle sighed. 'Everyone would, wouldn't they?'

'And what do you think?'

Danielle shrugged, wishing that Elaine would shut up. Her head was beginning to ache and she knew she had a full list to get through. 'I know what I'd like to think.'

'But you have doubts, like everyone else, is that it?'

'Something like that, yes.'

'Of course, if they are involved they won't be able to stay on the common.'

'Why? What do you mean?' Danielle looked up sharply.

'Well, you know what the brigadier said—he was happy for them to be there, provided they didn't break the law.'

Danielle took a deep breath. 'Elaine, I really must get on. Is Nathan in yet?'

'He came in, yes, then he was called straight out.'

She paused reflectively, her head on one side. 'It always happens, doesn't it?'

'What does?'

'What time was Maria Lees' baby born?'

'I'm not sure exactly; some time after midnight, I think. Why?'

'Well, Daphne Morrell died during the night.'

'Oh.' Danielle stopped as she thought about the family at the farm and how they must be feeling that morning.

'Dr Stafford's gone over there. Jack Morrell phoned and asked if he could visit.'

'Was it for the boy, Robert? I imagine he would be very upset.'

'No, surprisingly it was for Jill. She found her mother first thing this morning and apparently she just went to pieces.'

Danielle nodded. 'That's understandable. Jill had all the responsibility of the day-to-day care of her mother. She'll be lost now for a while.'

Somehow Danielle got through the rest of that sultry morning, only too aware, however, that practically every patient she saw in her clinic was buzzing with the rumours of the previous night. She only saw Nathan in passing, and he seemed distant and preoccupied.

As the day progressed her misery increased. It was as if the last few days hadn't happened and she and Nathan were back as they had been when they had first met, when he had appeared angry and uptight. The only bright spot in the day was when she phoned the hospital and was told that Maria and her baby were doing well, but even then the brief moment of happiness was dashed when Elaine rushed into her treatment-room just as she was clearing up.

'Guess what!' she demanded, her face red with excitement. 'That gypsy feller—you know, the big one—he's been taken in for questioning about the break-in at Foxworth.'

Danielle stopped what she was doing and, without turning from the dressing cupboard, said, 'You mean Rollo?'

'Yes, that's him.' Then she said curiously, 'Isn't he Maria's husband?'

Danielle nodded, still without turning. 'Yes, that's him.'

'Oh, dear, I should think that would cause a few problems,' said Elaine.

'Just a few.' Danielle angrily bit her lip and wondered if Rollo had been to the hospital before the police had caught up with him.

At the end of the afternoon, when she still hadn't seen Nathan to speak to, Danielle went to his consulting-room and tapped on the door.

When she entered the room he looked surprised, then a flicker of pleasure lit his blue eyes, to be quickly replaced by a look of what Danielle thought was embarrassment.

'I was wondering,' she said, 'if you wanted me to help you clear up the mess at Foxworth?'

'It's kind of you, Danielle, but I asked two women

from the village if they'd do it.' He glanced at his watch. 'They should be finished by now.'

'Oh, I see.' Danielle swallowed. Was this his way of telling her he didn't want her to go back to Foxworth with him? There was an awkward little silence, then Nathan cleared his throat.

'I'm sorry about your friend,' he began.

'You mean Rollo?' she said quickly, adding before he could answer, 'It was inevitable, really.'

He nodded as a low rumble of thunder sounded in the distance. 'Yes, I suppose so.'

'They'd be blamed for anything, whether they did it or not,' she said tightly.

His eyes narrowed. 'Are you saying you don't think he was responsible?'

She shrugged helplessly and shook her head. 'I don't know. . .I find it hard to believe he'd do anything like that.'

'He quite obviously didn't like me,' said Nathan quietly. A flash of lightning lit the room, closely followed by another rumble of thunder, louder this time. 'Either that or he didn't like my relationship with you.'

'My private life has nothing to do with Rollo,' said Danielle swiftly.

'Maybe someone should tell him that,' replied Nathan; then, taking a deep breath, he said, 'While we're on the subject, I think we need to talk about last night.'

Suddenly she couldn't bear to hear him say it had

all been a mistake. 'Oh, I don't think there's anything to discuss,' she said flippantly.

He stared at her, but before he could say any more she went on rapidly, 'I think we should simply put it down to a touch of summer madness, or maybe you were right and there was witchcraft about.' She gave a short, brittle laugh. 'Whatever it was, it's over. You'll be going back to Africa soon and we'll all get on with our lives.'

At that moment the telephone rang on Nathan's desk. There was another flash of lightning, and just before Danielle turned to hurry blindly from the room she saw the stricken look on his face.

He probably wasn't used to being spoken to like that by a woman, she thought, but later when she left the surgery her heart was heavy and she found herself wishing he'd never come to Lower Yarrow; then her life wouldn't have been turned upside-down.

The rain was just starting to fall, great thunder drops, and as Danielle ran across the green she decided she would collect her car and go to see Sophia.

Her thin cotton dress was wet by the time she unlocked her Morris Minor and scrambled inside, and as she drove through the village to the lane that led to the common the rain was quite deafening as it pounded on the roof of her car. All was quiet at Foxworth as she passed, and there was no sign of Nathan's car. Then she remembered that he was on call that night and the telephone call he had taken as she left his consulting-room had most likely been an emergency visit.

Allowing her thoughts to linger on him, she felt a stab of pain as she remembered the way it had been between them the previous day; their ride across the downs, that magical time at the ruined cottage, followed by his massage at Farthings, the way in which he had relaxed and opened up to her, and then the evening at Foxworth, which at the time she had been convinced was a prelude to their lovemaking.

Now it was all over. In a very short time he would walk out of her life, leaving her with only the memories of how he had aroused in her feelings she had never known existed, undreamt-of passion and desires.

With a sound like a sob she turned off the ignition and sat for a moment with her head resting on the steering-wheel.

At last, in a desperate attempt to pull herself together, she took several deep breaths, got out of the car and ran through the rain, her feet squelching on the soaking grass, until she reached Sophia's caravan.

When the gypsy woman opened the door Danielle was struck by how old and tired she looked.

'May I come in, Sophia?'

She stood aside and Danielle entered the caravan. A quick glance revealed that Sophia was alone. As the gypsy woman turned to her Danielle said, 'I came to see if you'd heard about Rollo.'

Sophia gave a helpless gesture and nodded. 'Yes,

he's still at the police station. I expect they've charged him by now.'

'Sophia. . .' Danielle hesitated, unsure how to continue '. . .do you blame me for this?'

'You? Why should I blame you?' Sophia frowned, then a cryptic little smile touched her lips. 'You mean because of you and your handsome doctor?' Danielle put out her hand in protest, but Sophia carried on. 'Rollo was jealous, I know that. I am his mother; I know how he is. We shouldn't have come here, it stirs too many memories. I told Rollo not to come, but he wouldn't listen.' She gave a deep sigh and sank down heavily on to her sofa.

'Sophia, you must believe me—there's nothing between Rollo and me.' Danielle paused. 'Oh, I don't deny that there might have been once, but that was a very long time ago, and I always knew it couldn't come to anything, just as Rollo did. He and Maria were always meant for each other.'

Sophia sighed again and nodded. 'Yes, and they both know it,' she said, 'and, whatever you might think, they really are fond of one another. . .'

'I'm sure they are. . .and they have their children.'

'It was just the memories, you see, of coming back here.'

'So you don't blame me?'

Sophia looked up at Danielle and patted the sofa beside her, then as she joined her she put one arm around her. 'Of course I don't blame you, little Dani—how could I? How could I blame you when Rollo is being blamed for something he didn't do?'

'He didn't?' Danielle drew in her breath sharply.

Sophia shook her head. 'He didn't come home until dawn. He'd walked into Pendleton, slept in a barn and walked back this morning. He knew nothing of the trouble at Foxworth, nothing of Maria's labour, not even the fact that he had a daughter. He had no time to get over any of it before the police came.'

'But didn't you tell them he hadn't been anywhere near the common?'

'Of course I told them, but come, now, Dani, you know better than that! Who would believe the word of a gypsy woman unless it suited them?'

'Oh, Sophia, it's so unfair! It always has been for you, for all of you. . .'

The older woman briefly tightened her grip on Danielle's shoulders, then she released her. 'Sometimes I think it's time I left the road,' she said. 'I'm getting older; even my powers aren't what they used to be. Maybe when all this is over I'll speak to Rollo about it. But what about you, Dani?' She turned again to Danielle. 'What about you and your doctor?'

'He isn't my doctor,' said Danielle, but there was a tremor in her voice as she said it, and she knew the gypsy woman noticed.

'Come on, Dani, you can't fool old Sophia. You and that man are made for each other. I may be losing some of my powers, but not that one. I know these things. . .have you ever known me to be wrong?'

Danielle smiled faintly and shook her head. 'No, I haven't,' she admitted, 'but there's a first time for everything, and I think this may be it.'

Sophia shook her head. 'I tell you, he's the man for you.'

'I don't see that it could ever work,' said Danielle miserably.

'Why? Is he married?'

'Only to his work.' She gave a rueful smile. 'His job is in Africa, caring for famine victims, and it seems to be the most important thing in his life.'

'I don't see the problem.' Sophia stood up and looked down at Danielle.

'Well, it could be difficult, with him in Africa and me here in Lower Yarrow.'

'So you go with him—I still don't see the problem. If you love your man you go where he goes.'

Danielle stared up at Sophia. 'You make it all sound so simple,' she said, shaking her head. 'I'm not even sure he'd want me with him.'

'You and this man of yours need to talk,' said Sophia firmly, then as Danielle stood up in preparation to leave she indicated for her to sit down again. 'No one leaves my home without I brew them some tea,' she said, her tone defying any argument.

The rain had eased a little by the time Danielle left Sophia, and she drove back to Farthings to find Shelley waiting for her on the window-sill. 'Well, you got in somewhere out of the rain, didn't you? You're beautifully dry,' she said as she stroked the cat, then unlocked the door and let them both in.

After she had eaten her supper she sat for a long time in her grandmother's old rocking-chair, thinking back over all Sophia had said. She knew how perceptive the gypsy woman was, even psychic over some things, and for a moment there, when she had said how sure she was that she and Nathan were meant for each other, Danielle's heart had pounded with excitement. Then she had remembered how distant he had seemed that day, almost as if he had regretted what had happened between them, and she knew the situation was hopeless. Suddenly she was glad they hadn't made love, because for her it would only have made their inevitable parting that much more difficult to bear. How he felt about it she still didn't know. At times she had been certain that he had felt the same way as her, but now she wasn't so sure. He had also been very angry about the break-in, and, whereas Sophia didn't blame her for what had happened, she had a feeling that Nathan in some way held her responsible because of her previous involvement with the gypsies, Rollo in particular.

As twilight deepened into night Danielle stood up and stretched, thinking it was time she went to bed and how she wouldn't be sorry to see the end of this particular day.

She was halfway up the stairs when the phone rang. She stopped in surprise, wondering who on earth could be phoning her at that time of night. She went back down the stairs and into the kitchen, and as she lifted the receiver she found herself hoping for one wild, unreasonable moment that it might be Nathan.

But it was Elaine's voice on the other end of the line.

'Danielle? Sorry it's so late, but George has just

come in from his crib game at the Crown and I thought you might like to know what he heard.'

'What's that, Elaine?' said Danielle, dreading what she could be about to hear next.

'They've released Rollo Lees.'

'*What*?' Danielle could hardly believe her ears.

'Yes. He had absolutely nothing to do with the break-in.'

'Well, I knew that, but how did he convince the police?'

'He didn't have to. George said old Hilton had come forward.'

'Old Hilton?' said Danielle in bewilderment. 'But surely he didn't have anything to do with it?'

'Oh, no, nothing like that. But he saw who did!'

'He did what?'

'Yes, it seems he was rabbiting in the woods. He saw you and Dr Stafford go with Maria in the ambulance, then a bit later he saw two youths go into Foxworth. Apparently he knew them both by sight, so he'll be able to make a positive identification.'

'Oh, Elaine, that's marvellous! Thank you so much for letting me know.'

'I thought you might have a better night's sleep if you knew your friends weren't to blame. You really are quite fond of them, aren't you?'

'Yes, Elaine, I am.'

'Well, I must get to bed now. I'll see you in the morning.'

'Goodnight. . .'

'Oh, there was just one other thing,' Elaine said

suddenly. 'If Maria Lees' baby was born after midnight, what were you doing going back to Foxworth with our handsome doctor in the wee small hours of the morning?'

'I'd left my keys there,' said Danielle.

'I suppose that's as good an excuse as any,' said Elaine with a chuckle as she hung up.

Danielle slept better than she thought she would, and when she awoke it was to a morning soft and fresh after the storms of the day before. As she showered and dressed, on a sudden impulse she decided to detour through the woods on her way to work and tell Sophia and Rollo, if he was there, how pleased she was that he had been cleared of suspicion.

An early-morning mist, slow to clear, hung wraith-like over the village green and curled between the trees as Danielle picked her way carefully across the wet grass, then along the muddy path through the woods.

The air felt fresh and smelt fragrant after the sultry, sticky heat, and Danielle drank in great lungfuls as she approached the common. She wondered if Rollo had been to see Maria and his new daughter. If he hadn't yet, because of all the trouble, surely nothing would stop him from going that morning.

She pushed her way through the last of the damp bracken, stepping over creeping bramble tendrils, then she stopped in bewilderment.

The common was empty.

The only signs that anyone had been there were the

areas of paler, flattened grass where the caravans had stood.

Wildly she stared around, unable to believe her eyes.

'I see you're as surprised as I was.'

She spun round and found Nathan standing behind her.

CHAPTER TWELVE

'NATHAN!' Danielle gasped, aware that her heart had turned over at the sight of him. 'Whatever's happened? Where have they gone?'

He shrugged. 'Your guess is as good as mine. I must admit, I never heard a thing in the night—for once I wasn't called out, so it wasn't until I got up that I realised they'd gone. Do you think they're on the run from the police?'

'No, it can't be that. Elaine phoned me late last night to say that she'd heard that Rollo had been released.'

Nathan raised his eyebrows in surprise. 'Why should he have been released?'

'Because it wasn't him. He didn't do it, Nathan, and they know who did.' Not giving him a chance to ask more questions, she quickly explained. 'Do you remember Sunday evening when we left Farthings, old Hilton was crossing the green with his dog?'

He nodded, then frowned. 'Yes, but I don't see what it has to do with him.'

'He was poaching in the woods and he saw who went into Foxworth after we'd gone to the hospital with Maria.'

His face tightened. 'So who was it?'

'Two youths, apparently. I don't know their names, but Hilton is able to identify them.'

Nathan stared at her, then let out a long breath. 'So,' he said at last, 'your friend wasn't to blame after all.'

Danielle shook her head. 'No, he wasn't.'

'I rather jumped to conclusions, didn't I?' He stared down at her, and at the look in his eyes she felt as if her bones were melting.

'Yes, you did,' she agreed. 'But then, people always do where the gypsies are concerned.'

'You must admit that your friend Rollo was jealous where you were concerned.

Danielle took a deep breath. 'Maybe he was, but that wasn't any fault of mine. As far as I was concerned, he was simply a friend, along with Maria and his mother.' Wildly she looked round at the empty common. 'And now they've gone, driven out again by suspicion, lies and gossip. And what of Maria and the baby?'

'We'll phone the hospital when we get to the surgery. Don't worry, they'll be all right.'

'Oh, I dare say they will, but it doesn't make me feel any better when I think how they've all been treated.' She gave a helpless, angry gesture.

He was silent for a long moment, then quietly he asked, 'Did you mean what you said yesterday that what happened between us was over?'

'It's for the best,' she said, blinking back the sudden tears that sprang to her eyes.

'I don't believe you mean that,' he said softly, resting his hands on her shoulders as he spoke, then placing his thumbs beneath her jaw, gently lifting her face until she was looking into his eyes.

'I thought you were regretting what had happened,' she said.

He frowned. 'Whatever gave you that idea?'

'I don't know. You seemed different somehow. . .'

'I was angry over what happened. . .'

'And I thought you were blaming me.'

'Of course I wasn't blaming you.' Hungrily his blue eyes searched her face, then before she could make any further protest he brought his mouth down on hers.

At first she tried to resist, then as she felt the treacherous betrayal of her body, the throbbing desire deep inside and the tingle of anticipation, she found herself responding with a passion that matched his.

At last when they pulled apart she clung to him. 'Oh, Nathan!' she cried, and it was almost a sob. 'Why is life so complicated?'

He didn't answer, but kept his arms around her, still holding her close, while she desperately found herself wishing that she was the most important thing in his life and not his work.

In the end it was she who finally pulled away, looking at her watch as she did so. 'Do you know, Dr Stafford,' she said in an attempt to sound light-hearted, 'we could find ourselves in trouble if we don't go now? We should have been in Surgery at least ten minutes ago.'

He groaned. 'OK, you win, but we'll resume this

conversation later. I think we have a few things we need to get straight.'

Like your going out of my life, after you've turned it upside-down, she thought miserably as they walked to his car.

When they reached the surgery it was to find Elaine almost bursting to tell them the latest news.

'Those two youths—they've been charged with the break-in,' she began excitedly, then she paused as the phone rang. 'It's for you, Dr Stafford,' she said a moment later. 'It's the police.'

'All right, Elaine, thank you; I'll take it in my room.' Nathan glanced at Danielle. 'Perhaps you'd like to ring the hospital?'

'Of course.' As Nathan disappeared to his room she turned towards her treatment-room, but Elaine called her back.

'Oh, don't go yet—I've got more to tell you.'

'If you mean about the gypsies vanishing in the night, I already know.'

'Did they? I didn't know that.' Elaine stared at her in astonishment. 'But where have they gone?'

Danielle shrugged wearily. 'You tell me.'

'But what about Maria and her baby?'

'That's what I have to ring the hospital about.' Once again she attempted to get to her room, and once again Elaine stopped her.

'I still haven't told you everything; listen: those two lads that were arrested, one of them works for Ralph Flint on his building sites and the other used to go out with Melanie Flint,' Elaine finished triumphantly. 'Now, what do you make of that?'

Danielle stared at her for a moment, lost for words, as she tried to grasp the implications of what Elaine had said. Then as several patients arrived for surgery and the receptionist's attention was taken she walked thoughtfully into her treatment-room and dialled the number of the local hospital. When the telephonist answered she asked to be put through to Obstetrics.

Moments later as she was replacing the receiver Nathan put his head round the door. He took one look at her face, then came right into the room, shutting the door behind him.

'What is it?' he demanded.

'That was the hospital.' She nodded towards the telephone. 'Maria Lees discharged herself and her daughter, against medical advice, in the early hours of the morning. According to the staff, her husband came for her, and he wasn't in any mood to argue. Oh, God, Nathan, I hope they'll be all right.'

'Well, they'll be miles away by now, so I don't see that there's any more we can do. Maria is in Sophia's hands now.'

'What did the police want?' She looked up sharply.

'Only to let me know that they'd arrested two persons in connection with the break-in at Foxworth. The curious thing is that the lads are adamant they didn't take anything, and that could quite well be true.' He paused. 'I certainly can't find anything missing. Although it may well be a different story when David and Judy return.'

'There certainly is something very strange going on,' admitted Danielle. 'Elaine's just told me that one of the lads works for Ralph Flint and the other used to go out with his daughter Melanie.'

'Ralph Flint, you say?' mused Nathan. 'There could be a link there, but I'm damned if I can work it out at the moment. All I know is I've got a waiting-room full of patients, and I really must get on.'

'Me too.' Danielle followed him out of the treatment-room to call her first patient, just as Dr Griffiths arrived in Reception.

He stared from one to the other with a totally bemused expression on his face. 'I wish someone would tell me what's going on,' he said tetchily.

'What do you mean, John?' Nathan paused as he was about to enter his room.

'Well, what's all this I've been hearing this morning—break-ins? Gypsies? Babies, and even something about old Hilton?'

Danielle, Nathan and Elaine stared at each other in amazement. Nathan found his voice first. 'You mean you really didn't know what's been happening, John?'

'I wouldn't be asking if I did,' he muttered. 'I'm supposed to be the senior partner around here, but no one tells me anything.'

'Tell you what, John,' said Nathan with a suppressed smile, 'Danielle and I will meet you for coffee if we ever get this morning's surgery done, then we can fill you in on what's been happening.'

It was, however, nearer to lunchtime when they

finally met in the staff-room and Nathan was able to give John Griffiths a brief outline of what had been happening.

'You say the police have charged someone?' Dr Griffiths asked.

Nathan nodded. 'At first it looked very much as if the gypsies were responsible, but now it seems as if it was the work of two local lads. Apparently one works for Ralph Flint.'

John Griffiths set down his cup and saucer and stared at Nathan. 'Ralph Flint, you say?'

'Yes,' Nathan nodded. 'Flint was the one who wanted the gypsies moved on in the first place. He even went to the trouble of contacting the brigadier in India.'

'Do you think he could have put those lads up to the break-in?' asked Danielle.

'I must admit, it had crossed my mind,' said Nathan. 'Maybe he did it because he knew the gypsies would be blamed.'

'Yes, and the brigadier had already said that they could only stay on the common provided they weren't breaking the law.'

'It makes sense,' said Nathan slowly. 'It would also explain why there was only damage done and nothing was taken. What I'm not sure about is why Flint was so set against the gypsies.'

'Oh, I know the reason for that,' said Dr Griffiths.

'You do?' They both stared at him as he leaned back in his chair and crossed his legs.

'Yes. I could have told you if you'd let me know

what was happening,' he said, and the same tetchy note that had been there earlier crept into his voice.

'Well, go on,' said Nathan. 'You can tell us now.'

Dr Griffiths glanced over his shoulder to make sure that what he was about to say would be in medical confidence. 'About ten days ago Ralph Flint's wife literally dragged their daughter here to see me. It appears her husband had gone home unexpectedly in the middle of the afternoon and had caught Melanie in bed with one of the gypsy lads. Apparently she'd had unprotected sex, and the mother was demanding everything from an AIDS test to the morning-after pill.'

'So that was it,' breathed Danielle. 'You remember we saw Melanie with one of the boys from the common, Nathan?'

'Yes, we commented at the time that her father wouldn't be too happy about it, not dreaming that he'd go to such lengths to get the gypsies out.'

'And it looks as if he's got what he wanted,' said Danielle bitterly. 'Even if he has to pay the fine for those two boys, the gypsies have gone, so Ralph Flint has won.'

At that moment there came a knock and Elaine put her head round the door. 'Sorry to interrupt,' she said, 'but there was a call for you during surgery, Dr Stafford—it was a Dr Garland from London. I told him you'd call him back. He said you'd know the number.'

'Oh, yes, Elaine, I know the number.' Nathan stood

up and looked down at the other two. 'Garland will want to know when I'm returning to the Sudan.'

Danielle felt her heart sink at his words, but before he had a chance to leave the room Elaine said, 'Oh, by the way, I thought you might be interested to know—the gypsies didn't leave on their own this morning.'

'What do you mean, Elaine?' asked Dr Griffiths.

'Melanie Flint went with them.'

There was silence in the staff-room, then Dr Griffiths found his voice. 'Melanie Flint is only fifteen, isn't she, Elaine?'

'No, Dr Griffiths, she was sixteen two days ago,' replied Elaine.

'In that case, I imagine her parents could have quite a job on their hands persuading her to return home,' said Dr Griffiths calmly.

After Elaine had left the room Nathan paused at the door, then with one hand on the door-handle he turned back to the other two. 'Did you say something about Flint having won, Danielle?'

She smiled, then, standing up, she smoothed down her uniform, ready to face the afternoon surgeries.

Danielle hardly saw Nathan again that afternoon, as she spent most of the time assisting Dr Griffiths with a health-promotion clinic. This included weight and blood-pressure checks on ten different patients, together with advice on smoking control, diets and cholesterol levels, alcohol abuse and the monitoring of individual problems like asthma, diabetes or chronic chest diseases.

In the end she left the surgery without knowing the outcome of Nathan's telephone call to the unknown Dr Garland and whether or not he had fixed a date for his return to Africa.

No doubt he was only too anxious to get back to his work, she thought as she walked across the green to her cottage. But would he remember her after he'd gone? Would he ever give a thought to that brief but ecstatic time they had shared, and if he did, would he merely dismiss it from his mind as just one of those pleasant encounters? Was that really all it had been to him?

By the time she got indoors she felt quite miserable and depressed, and she knew she was badly in need of some of her own aromatherapy.

She wasn't in the least bit hungry, so she went straight upstairs and ran herself a warm bath, then peeled off her clothes, dropping them on to the bedroom floor. Then, taking three phials from her glass cabinet, she went back into the bathroom and added two drops each of clary sage, bergamot and ylang-ylang to the running water.

With a sigh she lay back in the fragrant water, letting it lap softly over her body as she inhaled the aromatic vapours that she knew would lift her depresssion.

Half an hour later she stepped from the bath and wrapped herself in a thick, fluffy towel. As she padded through to her bedroom she thought she heard a sound downstairs, but, thinking it was Shelley, who had probably come in through the kitchen window, she took no notice. Sitting on the stool in front of her dressing-table, she allowed the towel to fall partially away, revealing her neck, shoulders and the swell of her breasts; then, picking up her hairbrush, she lowered her head and began to brush her hair forward from the roots.

The therapeutic movements seemed to revitalise her even further, then, as she flung her head back and lifted the brush to start again, a sudden movement caught her eye.

She glanced up, startled, and there, reflected in the mirror, in the open doorway of her bedroom stood Nathan.

She froze, the hand with the hairbrush poised as she stared at him, then instinctively she caught at the towel, drawing it closer around her.

He walked forward until he was standing directly behind her, then, leaning towards her, his eyes never once leaving hers in the mirror, he said, 'Don't do that.' Gently he pushed back the towel to its original position. 'You're beautiful, Danielle,' he said, his voice husky as he lowered his head and kissed the nape of her neck.

Suddenly she felt nervous, embarrassed even that he should catch her like this, and he, sensing it, said, 'I did knock, but you didn't hear. . .the door was open. . .' Then, lifting his head again, he said, 'That perfume. . .?'

'I put some oils in my bath,' she said softly. 'I was feeling tense and depressed.'

'And why was that?' he murmured, catching her hair and drawing it back from her face.

She lifted her shoulders slightly. 'I. . .I don't know.'

'Stay there,' he said, then turned and left the room.

A few minutes later he was back, and she saw he was carrying the small porcelain bowl she used to mix her essential oils.

'I would say today it's my turn to be therapist,' he said, and there was a hint of amusement in his voice as he gently drew the towel down so that it simply draped her waist and thighs. She watched, her senses heightened as he poured a little of the oils in his hands, rubbed them together, then moved them lightly, expertly, over her neck and shoulders.

At his touch Danielle arched her back, and her body responded as he dispelled any remaining shreds of tension; then she closed her eyes and blissfully gave herself up to the exquisite touch of his strong hands.

'How did you know which oils to use?' she asked dreamily at last.

'So which ones am I using?'

'Lavender and sandalwood?'

'Yes, and which other one?'

She hesitated. 'Geranium?'

'You do know your oils, don't you?'

'But how did you know which ones to use?' she persisted.

'Ah, I must confess, I looked it up just now in your

book. I simply found a formula for a relaxing massage and found the oils I wanted.'

'Well, it's certainly worked,' she said with a sigh as he finished.

'You still haven't said why you needed it in the first place.

'I told you, I was feeling depressed,' she said.

'I know, but you haven't told me why.'

'Maybe it had something to do with certain arrangements you had to make today,' she said at last, suddenly not caring what he might think of her.

'You mean my phone call to Garland?'

She nodded, raising her head so that once again her gaze met and held his. 'Something like that, yes.' This time her voice was barely more than a whisper. 'So when have you arranged to go?'

'Back to the Sudan?'

She nodded, then held her breath as that far-away look came into his eyes again that she had seen there before, and she knew he was seeing another world as far removed from her village existence as anything could possibly be.

'I told Garland my return was in some doubt,' he finally replied.

Danielle felt her body tense. 'Why did you say that?'

'Because I don't think I shall be able to return.'

Her pulses suddenly began to race. 'But it's your whole life.'

'I know. It was everything to me.'

'Was?'

'Yes, was. Until something more important happened. Until someone came along, someone special whom I shall find impossible to leave.'

Still not taking her eyes from his in the reflection in the mirror, she lifted her arms above her head, and as he leaned over her she drew his head down, then turned her face so that her lips met his.

He carried her into the bedroom, the towel falling to the floor as he lifted her in his arms. His breath caught in his throat as he had his first glimpse of her supple body, her smooth, satiny skin, the high, firm breasts, the slim waist and softly rounded hips tapering to her long golden-brown legs.

Gently he lowered her on to the down-filled duvet with its white embroidered cover, the cotton pillows edged with broderie anglaise, delicately scented with her own jasmine-perfumed oils.

Danielle watched him as he undressed, secure now in the knowledge that he loved her and wanted her to the point that he couldn't bear to leave her. As the last of his garments fell to the floor he lowered himself on to the bed above her, his hard suntanned body aroused and ready to prove his love for her.

He was gentle, as she had known he would be, caressing and murmuring words of love as he claimed her, then as he neared his own point of fulfilment growing more demanding, while she reached a level of awareness she had never known before.

When it was over they lay in each other's arms, and Danielle studied Nathan's profile, as with his head half turned away from her he gazed towards the open window. She sensed rather than saw that the distant expression was back in those blue eyes and knew she had to say now what she was thinking if she was not to spend the following months and years wondering if he had regrets.

'Nathan?' she said softly, reaching out her hand and gently stroking the side of his face.

'Yes, my love?' He turned his head and smiled at her, then, catching her hand, he pressed it to his lips, kissing each of her fingers in turn.

'I don't think you'll be able to exist without your work in Africa,' she said.

He sighed. 'I might have thought that once, but what we've just shared has convinced me that I can't exist without you.' Lowering his head, he dropped gentle kisses on her face, her cheeks, her eyelids and the tip of her nose, moving then to her neck, the vulnerable hollow of her shoulder, which made her squirm with renewed delight, then finally the hardening tip of her breast.

Desperately trying to concentrate on what had to be said, but only too conscious that she was losing the battle as her senses yielded to his growing demands, Danielle drew a deep breath. 'Has it occurred to you that you could have both?'

Nathan stopped the sensuous explorations of his mouth and for a moment was perfectly still. At the window the soft evening breeze gently lifted the chintz curtains, stirring the jasmine aroma, revitalising the senses; then he lifted his head and looked at her.

'What do you mean?'

While he had been kissing her his left hand had been gently caressing, stroking the smooth skin of her thighs, but this too he now stopped, his hand resting on her hip as he stared at her.

'I would have thought the solution was simple,' she said.

He frowned. 'I don't understand.'

'I come with you.' As she said it Sophia's words hovered at the edges of her mind; if you love your man you go where he goes.

Nathan caught his breath, and the hand on her hip tightened its grip. 'I couldn't ask you to do that, Danielle.'

'You haven't asked me. I said I'd go.'

He shook his head. 'You don't understand. It's a tough world; it's not the sort of thing I'd ask a woman to share.'

'Aren't you forgetting something?'

'What's that?'

'I'm a nurse as well as a woman. I would imagine trained nurses are needed out there?'

'Well, yes. . .but. . .'

'But what?' she arched her eyebrows.

Helplessly he lifted his shoulders. 'This place—the cottage, Lower Yarrow. . .I didn't think in a million years you'd ever want to leave it.'

'I would never sell this cottage,' she said firmly.

'I must admit, it would be the perfect place to come home to. . .'

'So is that settled, then?' She smiled up at him. 'Good—well, in that case, please can you now carry on with what you were doing?' As she spoke she turned and pressed her body against his.

With an exclamation of undisguised delight he put his arms round her, drawing her even closer and leaving her in no doubt about his immediate intentions.

DON'T MISS EUROMANCE

1992 is a special year for European unity, and we have chosen to celebrate this by featuring one Romance a month with a special European flavour.

Every month we'll take you on an exciting journey through the 12 countries of the European Community. In each story the hero will be a native of that country–imagine what it would be like to be kissed by a smouldering Italian, or wined and dined by a passionate Frenchman!

Our first **EUROMANCE**, *'The Alpha Man'* by Kay Thorpe is set in Greece, the land of sunshine and mythology. As a special introductory offer we'll be giving away *'Hungarian Rhapsody'* by another top author, Jessica Steele, absolutely free with every purchase of *'The Alpha Man'*.

And there's more . . .

You can win a trip to Italy simply by entering our competition featured inside all Romances in September and October.

Published: September 1992 Price: £1.70

Available from Boots, Martins, John Menzies, W.H. Smith, most supermarkets and other paperback stockists. Also available from Mills & Boon Reader Service, PO Box 236, Thornton Road, Croydon, Surrey CR9 3RU.

Mills & Boon